THE DEVIL'S DICTIONARY

A new collection of six tales of dark fantasy by a master storyteller:

An occult scholar obtains an ancient grimoire and uses it to summon up the Devil…

Three tramps find a metal vessel akin to Aladdin's Lamp and release a Jinn who grants them a wish they might come to regret…

The excavation of an ancient dolman releases an imprisoned evil…

Could anyone trust the proprietor of the strange little shop who claimed to be a dealer in dreams?

The mission of mercy that caused a space traveller to disappear…

What happens when a man's memories are utterly destroyed?

Fascinating reading by a master of the weird tale!

ALSO BY E.C. TUBB

Assignment New York: A Mike Lantry Classic Crime Novel
Enemy of the State: Fantastic Mystery Stories
Galactic Destiny: A Classic Science Fiction Tale
The Ming Vase and Other Science Fiction Stories
Mirror of the Night and Other Weird Tales
Only One Winner: Science Fiction Mystery Tales
Sands of Destiny: A Novel of the French Foreign Legion
Star Haven: A Science Fiction Tale
Talk Not At All: Science Fiction Stories
Tomorrow: Science Fiction Mystery Tales
The Wager: Science Fiction Mystery Tales
The Wonderful Day: Science Fiction Stories

THE ATILUS TRILOGY

1. *Atilus the Slave*
2. *Atilus the Gladiator*
3. *Atilus the Lanista*

THE DEVIL'S DICTIONARY

Weird Fantasy Tales

E.C. TUBB

Edited by Philip Harbottle

WILDSIDE PRESS

Published by Wildside Press LLC.
www.wildsidebooks.com

CONTENTS

THE DEVIL'S DICTIONARY

I saw the book on the second-hand counter of Manlick's bookstore. It was tucked away among a lot of popular trash and the bound files of out-of-date magazines. At first I thought that it was a bible, one of the thick, leather-bound affairs which used to be popular years ago when they were used more as a family record than as a book of comfort and guidance. Then I picked it up and riffled the pages and immediately knew that I had found what I had been looking for.

Not the book itself, of course, but any book that was a bargain. You don't get many of them nowadays, though the odd item is still to be picked up from where it is hidden among rubbish. Most booksellers check their stock pretty thoroughly so that there are slim pickings for the expert to find. I am an expert in a small way, at least I can tell the first editions from the reprinted copies, the rare works from those which look good but are valueless, and I can date a book as well as the next man.

The book I was holding was old.

The paper was the thick, heavy, hand-made kind you just don't get now. The lettering was the black-text style with the cursives and flourishes that Caxton first introduced when he set up shop from the continent. The text was, of course, in Latin, and several pages had been hand-illuminated with gold leaf and colourful pigments.

I can read a little Latin and what I read made me all the more determined to purchase the volume. Manlick was watching me, it doesn't take long for a bookseller to classify his customers, and his little eyes narrowed as I showed him the book.

"How much for the relic?"

"Relic?" He took it, flipped the pages, and pretended to know more than he did. "Where did you find it?"

"Down with the junk." I took the book from his hands and opened the front cover. "No price marked. Five pounds?"

We argued, of course, but he didn't really know what the book was worth and I knew he couldn't read Latin.

We settled for ten pounds after I had shown him the scarred binding and the mildewed pages and lied about how much it would cost to restore the book to a decent condition. After the sale he relaxed a little and I asked him from where the book had come.

"It's part of a library I bought from Sir Clement's estate." He shrugged. "You know how these libraries are. Plenty of Victorian stuff, some good first editions, a mess of rubbish and one or two really good items. That book must have been among the rubbish. I had Winslow sort the stuff out for me and he's a good man."

He was, too good, and I wondered just how he had let this item slip past his shrewd evaluation of the worth of any book ever printed. I didn't let it worry me, finding old books is similar to a treasure hunt, quite often the regular search is a waste of time but occasionally the rewards are high.

Back home I unwrapped my prize and gave it a closer examination.

Dating it was hard because there was neither printer's imprint or date of publication but I placed it as mid-seventeenth century. I had been right about the hand-illumination, someone had illustrated the book with gold-leaf and pigments and, looking at it, I was reminded of the old manuscripts of the past. That dated it still further because the tendency after printing first became introduced was to copy the old manuscripts as far as possible.

If it hadn't been for the faint impression of the type on the reverse side of the paper, the elaborate cursives and gothic text, I'd have thought that the entire missal had been hand-produced.

I managed to read two pages, struggling with the Latin and frowning over the blurred type. Two pages were enough. I had read just enough to know that what I had found was no ordinary book of prayer or sermons There was something vaguely disquieting in the hints contained in the introduction but my knowledge of the dead language wasn't good enough for me to do more than gain a hint at what the book contained.

I decided to take it to Henshaw.

George Hemshaw was a recluse who had bound himself with books and dead knowledge. I had met him one day while making some researches at the British Museum and, from a casual nodding acquaintanceship, we had become as close as two people of naturally reserved natures could be. He lived on the top floor of an old rambling house bequeathed to him by a dead aunt, one of those horrible Georgian style houses still to be seen in some parts of the city, and the lower part of the house was filled with the most indescribable collection of curios I have ever seen outside of a museum.

I had heard whispers about George from those who should have known what they were talking about. As a young man he had travelled the world and spent much time m Tibet. Back in London he had become involved with a cult of Satanists and, for a time, had lived on the thin edge of the law. There had been a nasty expose concerning the death of a young man at a ceremony and George, disgusted with the aims and objects of the cult, had withdrawn from all association with them.

That didn't concern me. What did interest me was that George had an astounding knowledge of Latin and his collection of old books of a specific nature was unequalled by any man or institution in the country. If anyone could tell me just what it was that I had found it would be he.

"It's old," he admitted after I had shown him my prize. "Where did you say it came from?"

"Sir Clement's library. Manlick must have bought the lot cheap and had Winslow check them for him. How Winslow ever came to overlook this I shall never know." I smiled as I touched the old, cracked leather of the binding. "Lucky for me he did, though."

"Winslow is a religious man," he said absently. "I'm only surprised that he didn't destroy the book." He stared at me, his thin face serious in the fading light of day. I smiled at his expression.

"Burn it? Why should he have done? And what has his being a religious man to do with it?"

"There is some knowledge better lost," George said quietly. "Not because, in itself, it is bad, but for the misuse which may be made of it by others. This book," again he rested his hand on the scarred cover, "contains such knowledge."

"Please." I was a little annoyed at my friend and impatient to discover the book's true worth. A staunch materialist, I had little patience with those who hinted at mysterious knowledge and hidden secrets. Such tales were, for me, the vapid outpourings of diseased minds. I picked up the book and opened it at the introduction.

"Let's get down to it. From what I can make out it was written by a monk, and printed in the mid-seventeenth century. Now, there is something odd right away. The monasteries were dissolved by then and few if no books were produced by monks at that time. Certainly they weren't printed." I looked at George. "I'd say that this volume is a copy of an earlier work. Would you agree?"

He didn't answer straight away but, taking the book, switched on a desk lamp and held the open page in the cone of brilliance. For a long time he read the awkward text, his lips moving silently as he followed the Latin, then he looked up at me with an expression that contained both anticipation and surprise.

"You are right," he said. "The original was written late in the twelfth century by a monk of the Franciscan Order, a Brother Shwartz of Berthanbolm, in a monastery buried deep in the Hartz mountains. The introduction gives his history and makes it quite plain that the Brother was burned for heresy and dabbling in the black arts." George leaned back in his chair, his thin hands resting on the book, his eyes behind their thick lenses serious.

"In short, John, you have found a copy of an authentic Grimoire, a handbook for witches and wizards."

"Is that all?" I was disappointed. Grimoires, while of interest to those concerned with old fables and magic spells, had only a limited market. I had hoped that the book would prove to be of more general interest. I held out my hand for the volume but George was reading on and seemed not to have noticed my gesture. So deep was his concentration that I left him and busied myself with studying some of his collection. I had seen his books before but now, for the first time, I noticed that, masked by harmless-looking covers, many of them were similar works to the one I had found. Grimoires of Black and White magic, books of spells and incantations, many of them with intricate diagrams and long lists of formula for magic potions. I was reading a recipe for the making of a Glory Hand, the dismembered hand of a corpse treated in a special way and which was said to have the power of opening all locks, when a sudden exclamation from my friend caused me to close the book and stare at him.

"What is it, George?"

"This is wonderful!" There could be no mistaking his enthusiasm. "John! Do you realise what you have found?"

"An old book on Black Magic," I said. "Why?"

"This is one of the genuine volumes which escaped the great burning of the dark ages." George was really excited. "The text explains just how it came to be in print. It seems that a small group of practitioners, persecuted and hounded by the Church and the civil authorities, disbanded their libraries and buried most of their works. Some of them, however, tried a second way to preserve the forbidden knowledge. They chose to do it by multiple records. They bribed a printer to produce a thousand copies of the book and intended to spread them among the initiated over the then-known world. It was a good plan and might well have succeeded but for the faint-heartedness of the printer. He informed the authorities and the entire stock of books, together with the original manuscript and the galley-proofs were destroyed. This book, obviously a proof to be checked against the final production, is the only one to have survived. Naturally, the illuminations and binding were added later."

"So we have the rarest of First Editions," I said interestedly. "One single copy of one single print-order. It should be worth quite a sum."

"It is," he said, and hesitated. "How much were you thinking of asking, John?"

It was my turn to hesitate. If the book was as rare as he said then I could ask my own price from those collectors interested in such things. It might even be worth my while to offer it to the British Museum or to the institutions abroad. Against this was my friendship with George who obviously wanted the volume for himself. I tried to find a middle way.

"I don't want to rob you, George, but at the same time, not having a private income as you have, I want to make as much as I can."

"I'll give you twenty thousand pounds," he said curtly. "Well?"

Again I hesitated. Twenty thousand pounds was, to me, a lot of money.

"How about if I had it photocopied, George? You would then have an authentic copy and it wouldn't cost you anywhere near as much?"

"No." He smiled at me and I recognised the light of the collector gleaming in his eyes. I had seen it before and knew that, no matter how much I asked, he would do his best to raise the sum. "Thank you, John, but no. It wouldn't be the same. Twenty-five thousand and that's my top figure."

"I'll take the twenty thousand," I said. "If you want it that badly I can't refuse you."

He smiled and wrote me out a cheque without hesitation and, after I had folded it and put it in my pocket, he picked up the book again as though he couldn't bear to be parted from it.

"I suppose you think I'm a little insane, John," he said quietly. "Maybe I am, but to me this book is worth all I own."

"As a collector's item?" I smiled and shook my head. "It can be an expensive hobby, George."

"Yes and no," he said seriously. "I know you, John, and know that you are a strict materialist. You don't believe in this sort of thing, do you?"

"Black Magic?" I shook my head. "Childish superstitions born in ignorance and fed by the unthinking faith of the illiterate."

"And the Alchemists?"

"Bunglers." I smiled at his expression. "Oh, I know that they are supposed to have been the early chemists and that, in their way, they tried to make honest discoveries. But the few things they did discover, gunpowder for example, were due to accident. They filled their experiments with verbal rubbish and appeals to non-existent spirits and demons. But what did they really do to help modern knowledge?"

"There are two ways of attacking any problem," he said quietly. "Much of the old science is, as you say, rubbish, but not all." He relaxed in his chair and stared at me through his thick glasses.

"Sorcery in the Middle Ages was highly questionable. The average egoist was an outright charlatan. Some wizards hung around the courts of small nobles or petty princes, dabbling in astrology, palmistry and a little alchemy. They were totally un-genuine. Others were like modern confidence tricksters, forever asking for money to perfect their experiments in order to find the Elixir of Youth or the Philosopher's Stone with which to transmute base metals into gold. A third class were quack doctors, men who ran little shops in side streets and sold false love philters and who promised to put curses and spells on enemies. They, like the others, were also dishonest in that they could not do as they claimed.

"Mixed in with these impostors were the psychopathic cases. Demoniacs and diaboleptics who pranced naked on the hilltops during Walpurgis Eve and who claimed to be in communication with the Devil. There we have the clear evidence of inverted religious mania. Remember the Dancing Hysteria which swept over Europe at the time of the

Crusades? But always there were serious students of the mantic arts. From their records, hidden as they are with allusion and symbolism, we, those of us who are interested, are trying to rediscover just what it was they knew."

"But did they really know anything?" I admitted his sincerity but could not feel it myself. George nodded.

"Yes." He smiled at my expression. "Don't take my word for it. Science now recognises the pathological existence of the werewolf and vampire in mental cases. Science now recognises many practises today that once were labeled as witchcraft. The search for the Philosopher's Stone is one. We now transmute mercury into gold by the medium of the cyclotron. In the old days they also thought that they could change mercury into gold, but they tried it with heat and spells and incantations."

"That's different," I said quickly. "That's science."

"What is science but the search for the truth?" he said evenly. "No, John, you can't damn all those old seekers after knowledge because they tried a different method than ourselves. True, they used to brew a mixture containing toads and foxgloves for heart troubles. Now we know that both toads and foxgloves contain digitalis—used now for the treatment of heart disease."

He rose and crossed to his shelf of old volumes.

"Collected here, John, are the fruits of those early seekers after knowledge. A lot of it is rubbish that I grant, still more is hopelessly shrouded in allusion and symbolism, but there was a good reason for that. Remember the times in which they were written, John. There was no tolerance then. Heresy earned death at the stake and anyone not following the strict line laid down by the Church was deemed a 'heretic.' They had to be vague for their own protection. But I believe that they stumbled on things since lost to us. For hundreds of years men tried to find a path to knowledge and power. Riddled with superstition as they were, yet is it asking too much to believe that they may have learned something from all their experiments? That is what I hope to prove and, now that I have your book, there is no need for further delay."

"So the book was important then?" Almost I regretted selling it. George nodded.

"Yes. The writer of that book had done a tremendous amount of research and had correlated his findings in what, we would call now, a scientific way. In effect it is what we would call a dictionary of scientific terms. The ancients had their terminology, you know, and not all of it meant what it appears to mean. With the book as a guide I am sure that we can conduct certain experiments with a fair degree of success."

He meant it. He believed that he spoke nothing but the simple truth and, as I stared at him, I felt the first stirrings of excitement. I forced myself to appear calm.

"Do you actually mean to tell me that you think you can conjure up demons and spirits from the nether-world?"

"Did I say that?" He shrugged with the impatience of a man who has long been accustomed to misunderstanding. "Let me repeat; the ancients tried a different path to knowledge. Where we depend on a frontal attack, force if you like, they tried to obtain their results by appealing or demanding aid from either the matter itself or from other-world entities. Don't scoff, John. If you had seen what I have seen…"

He broke off and I remembered his dabblings in the occult. I smiled and reached for my hat.

"Very well, George, I won't scoff, but one thing I'd like you to promise. When you get ready to conduct your experiments I'd like to be in on them. Agreed?"

He hesitated, then nodded. "Agreed."

I left him busy reading the old volume I had just sold him for twenty thousand pounds.

It was a month before I heard from George again. I heard of him from mutual acquaintances and one day I bumped into Fred Brown, an old bibliophile who knew as much about books as I did and whose collection of first editions was the envy of most of his friends. We had a drink together and over a small table in a secluded booth, he mentioned George.

"What's he up to?" Fred grinned at me though his eyes were sharp. "I've heard that he's getting mixed up with some of his old friends again. Frank tells me that he was in the old apothecary's, you know that herbalists in Market Street, when he saw George collect an order. Dragon's Blood, powdered Mandrake, dried Mummy and dessicated toads as well as a lot of other stuff. Is George up to his Devil Worship again?"

"Not as far as I know." I dismissed the incident with a shrug. "From what I heard he wants to try some old recipes he found in an old Grimoire."

"Black Magic!" Fred shuddered. "The fool! He doesn't know what he's letting himself in for."

"Do you?" I'd heard rumours about Fred and, though I liked the man, yet there was something reptilian about him. He grunted.

"Maybe I do and maybe I don't, that's neither here nor there. But if you're a friend of his you'll do your best to stop him messing about with powers he can't control or understand. Remember Sam Young?"

I blinked at the sudden change of subject.

"Why?"

"Never mind, why? Do you remember him or not?"

"Yes, I remember him." I did too. Sam Young had been an artist of the modern school. That is he starved while bewailing the fates that prevented his genius from being acknowledged. Now that Fred mentioned it I hadn't seen Sam for more than two years. I said as much.

"I'm not surprised," said Fred grimly. "He's kept locked up now and has been ever since his breakdown. Went stark, staring mad one night and tried to kill his landlady. They caught him in time, certified him, and put him away where he couldn't do any harm." He leaned closer to me and lowered his voice. "Sam tried messing about with old recipes. They say he was smeared all over with some kind of cream when they caught him. Why, I don't know, but he was seen shopping for much the same ingredients as your friend just before his breakdown." He winked at me. "A word to the wise..."

I nodded and sat for a long time over my drink after Fred had left. I hadn't given it much thought up till now. George's money had made life very easy for me and I had been busy tasting a little of the luxury I had always wanted but had never been able to afford. Now, because of what Fred had said, I began to feel a certain responsibility towards my friend and, leaving my drink unfinished on the table, I rose and headed for the British Museum. There were certain parchments that I wanted to consult as well as certain things I felt that I should obtain. Fred, despite his reputation, was a man I felt I could trust.

It was exactly five days later that George sent for me.

He was changed in a way I found hard to describe. He wasn't thinner than usual or gaunt or wasted. It was as if he had just awakened from sleep and was full of energy and enthusiasm. He met me at the door of his house and, as the portal closed behind me, thunder rippled over the darkened city and a brief flash of lightning illuminated his face through the transom. It died and the soft glow of candles replaced the electric fury. I looked at them.

"What's the matter with the lights, George?"

"They fused an hour ago." He led me upstairs, talking all the time. "Sorry to have sent for you so late, John, but I'm all ready to begin." He chuckled, a sound of genuine anticipation and good humour. "I suppose you're going to say why not wait until tomorrow, but why? I'm eager to get started and the sooner the better." He opened the door and led the way into his study where, as I stripped off my overcoat, he sat down and poured out two glasses of wine.

"Thanks." I sipped the wine and jumped as thunder shook the old house. "A fine night for what you have in mind."

"The thunder?" He shrugged. "That isn't important. I doubt if the electrical content of the air will affect the formula in any serious way. The astrological predictions are just right, however. Mercury is in transit and Venus is in trine. The House of…"

"Please!" I held up my hand. "You're talking Greek to me, I'm no astrologer. Is it important?"

"I don't know," he admitted. "It could be. I'm trying to think of the whole thing as a series of scientific experiments. The trouble is that we aren't too sure of what is important and what isn't. It is much like mixing a chemical formula, some things are indispensable, others can be added without real harm. Only, instead of measurable quantities of chemicals we are dealing with vibrations, angles, gases and combinations of intangibles any of which might be the key factor."

He saw my expression and laughed.

"Don't look so bewildered, John. After all it was your book which provided the answer to my search."

"But isn't it filled with the same fake gibberish as all the rest?"

"No."

"Look," I insisted. "I've read some of that stuff and it usually doesn't make any sort of sense at all."

"True, but there are kernels of truth and, never forget that most of it is illusion and symbolism. That is why the book you sold me is so important. It defines terms and quantities so as to make them understandable." He sighed as he stared at me: "Suppose, for example, you knew nothing of modern chemistry and found a formula for the making of gunpowder. It would read: Charcoal, fourteen percent; sulphur, ten percent; potassium nitrate, seventy-five per cent; water, one per cent. Understandable? To you now, perhaps, but how about to one of the old alchemists? He wouldn't know what 'per cent' meant and he would never have heard of potassium nitrate or sulphur. Convert the terms into his own terminology and you'd have something he could understand."

"Charcoal, fourteen parts," I said understandingly. "Brimstone, ten parts; saltpetre, seventy-five parts and moisten with water." I nodded.

"And the reverse applies," George said impatiently. "What did the old alchemists mean when they referred to 'The breath of the green dragon'? Some things we know are false, for example we know that any formula necessitating the powdered horn of Unicorn must mean something entirely different. Rhinocerous horn perhaps? Certainly not Unicorn, we know now that there is no such animal." He glanced at his wristwatch and listened as thunder rolled overhead. "No, John. Some of the spells are frauds; others are genuine."

"You mean that if you read a spell aloud it would conjure up a demon?"

"If you read it correctly," said George. "That's the whole point and that is why we are here tonight, to find out the truth if possible within the framework of scientific experiment." He tilted his head as a knock sounded from the door downstairs and, with a muttered apology, he left me to admit his guest.

I had never met Martin Lamas before and found him most interesting to look at. A thin, dried up little man with a head almost too big for his body and a trick of washing his hands as he spoke. His worn clothing revealed his poverty and, as he grinned and sipped at his wine, I was conscious of his eyes, small and sharp like those of a bird, flickering around the snug study as if in search of something.

"We were talking of reading spells," said George. "That is why I invited Martin to take a part in our experiment. You know, of course, that all the old incantations are written in Latin. You also know that, no one now knows just how the Latin was pronounced. We can read it, talk it, but we do not know how the original Romans sounded their syllables. It is as if an American were to read an English essay. It would sound recognisable but there would be stress placed on the wrong vowels and, as far as the vibrations went, it would sound totally different." George leaned forward. "The vibrations, John! That is the whole secret of the old incantations! The words themselves mean nothing, it is only the vibrations set up in pronouncing them which is important. That is why most of the spells read like ridiculous gibberish. Can you understand?"

"Yes," I said, and I did. "You are saving that the vibrations may act on the intangible plane separating us from the Unknown in the same way as a certain tone may affect the sonic-lock of a door. We could set the lock of such a door to open only to a series of notes of music or vibrations of sound. Any words that gave the correct sounds would do. Any words—if spoken correctly. A lock set to the English phrase 'Pass the Tomato', would fail to open if an American spoke the words because he would use the short instead of the long 'a'."

"Exactly." George seemed pleased. "Any words. Perhaps the well-known phrase 'Open Sesame' had some such original significance, but we wander from the point. Martin here, as far as anyone can tell, is the only man now capable of speaking Latin with the original pronunciation. At least, he says that he is, maybe we shall find out for sure tonight."

Thunder rolled as the little man nodded and sipped at his wine. Unaccountably I shivered and, even as I did so, wondered why.

We sat and talked and drank wine until it was almost midnight and then George led us downstairs to the big, un-used dining room of the old house. When I had last seen it, it had been filled with heavy, old-fashioned furniture, but now it was empty, with heavy drapes hanging from the ceiling and against the walls. Some equipment stood on the parquet floor and, on a table pushed against one wall, jars and boxes rested with sticks of chalk and rolled parchments.

"These are our ingredients," said George. "Corpse fat candles and phosphorescent chalk. Blood, I bought that from a man I know, and other things all of interest and, if I may say so, all very hard to obtain nowadays. Still," he chuckled, "it's surprising how easy it is to get the most out of things when it is possible to pay for them. And all genuine and guaranteed, even to the dried Mummy and powdered toadstools." He drew a deep breath. "Now, John, and you too Martin, let us be serious. This is in the nature of an experiment and we must approach it exactly as we would any other experiment. If we are successful we may open doors to knowledge undreamed of. Wealth, fame, power; if only a part of what the ancients believed comes true, then we shall have the world at our feet."

Martin nodded and, even though I still felt the faint superciliousness of a man who knew quite well that all this was but make-believe, I too became serious. I became more than that. I became as acutely interested as George himself for, if by some incredible chance the experiment should work, then, as he had said, we should have control of powers unknown in the world today.

Intently I watched him prepare for the ritual.

On the smooth floor he traced a pentagram with the chalk, which glowed with an evil blue light of its own.

A small fire was lit in a brazier and candles, thick and odoriferous, set around the pentagram. Strange, cabalistic signs were traced with red and green and yellow pigments and a convoluted spiral writhed around the pentagram and symbols as if it were a serpent swallowing its own tail.

"The pentagram is the focus, as you might call it," said George. "I've made certain that it is mathematically correct and that the angles are as specified. The symbols also are said to have a restraining influence and the outer ring should bolster them so as to provide a measure of safety against anything which we may conjure up." He moved around outside the circle and iron rubbed against the polished wood.

"Cold iron is also said to be a guard against demons," said George. He dabbed at his face and I noticed that he was sweating. "The incantation I have chosen for this experiment is Abbot Richalmus's spell to call up a draconibus. It is clearly laid out in his *Liber Revelationum de Insidia et Versutiis Daemonum Adversus Homines*. It is supposed to be a very effective spell and, now that we have the knowledge from the new Grimoire, I think that we can hope for success."

"Wait a moment. I thought that you were going to call up the Devil," I said. "What's a draconibus?"

"A flying cacodemon of the night," said George shortly. "What made you think I intended to call up Satan?"

"Why not?" The fumes from the candles, or it may have been the wine, had made me a little light-headed. "If we want power isn't he the one to give it to us?"

"Perhaps, but obviously you have forgotten what you have learned." George was surprisingly abrupt. "Satan never gives anything for nothing. If he gives you something be sure that it will cost you dear in the end." He glanced at his wrist. "Enough of talk. Are we ready?"

Martin nodded and picked up a scroll, one of several lying on the table. I nodded and stepped back against the wall, my hand in my pocket, my eyes watchful. George, after a last examination of the pentagram, scooped something from a box and crossed to a brazier.

And then everything began to grow unreal.

I saw him cast something on the flames and a flaring gout of colour rose towards the ceiling and painted the room with flickering shades of red and green and yellow. The fires died and thick, incense-like smoke welled from the brazier and dimmed the guttering light of the candles. Outside the thunder rolled as if to a fiendish accompaniment to the work inside the old house and, as it snarled about us, I saw Martin unroll his scroll and begin to read.

And then I became afraid.

I had never believed that human tongue could utter such sounds. The Latin, but a Latin I had never before heard, rolled from his throat in a jarring harmony of vibration and, as it swelled around us, I saw George, his face a perspiring mask, move swiftly about the room. He threw powders onto the brazier and smoke and colours blossomed beneath his hands. Liquid gurgled from a flask and my nostrils twitched to the scent of burning blood. He scattered perfume and strange spices into the pentagram and, all the time he worked, the little man's voice rose louder and louder until it seemed that all the city would be able to hear him above the noise of the storm.

And yet I knew that it was only a local illusion. It wasn't that Martin's voice had really risen louder but that the sounds he was uttering had taken on a peculiar penetrating quality. They acted as the screech of a nail against a slate or the droning sub-harmonics of a dentist's drill played on the nerves. It seemed to me that the power and tension within the room would soon burst beyond the walls and spill out into the street and, faintly behind me from the direction of the table, I heard the splinter of glass as a phial shattered beneath the ghastly vibrations which seemed almost able to tear soul from body.

The tension mounted, higher, higher, and then, with something like an unearthly scream, the little man threw back his head and, together with the snarling crack of thunder, shouted the last line of the hellish incantation set down by a man long dead.

Silence. A silence which was heavy with the coiling after-echoes of thundering vibrations and the subdued pulse of unimagined terrors. The air was thick with smoke and incense, nauseating with odours from the various powders George had flung into the brazier, and sickly with the scent of the corpse fat candles.

Silence—and that was all.

How long I stood there, my hand tight around the thing in my pocket, my lips pressed tightly together so that the muscles of my face ached from the strain I shall never know. I stared into the smoke and the haze and, it may have been imagination or it may have not, but it seemed to me as if something writhed in the smoke and moved so that the drifting clouds took on a squat and horribly human form. I blinked and shook myself as the curtains rattled back from the windows and the cold night air dispersed the smoke.

"We failed," said George dully. "The incantation didn't work."

He snapped the light switch and cursed when no lights appeared. I, in order to get away from the fog, offered to repair the fuse and when I had done so rejoined them in the big room. In the harsh electric light the brazier and chalk marks on the floor seemed the foolish playthings of children and it was hard to believe that I had cringed with terror beneath the vibrations of a voice and the unseen, but tangible hint of an unearthly presence.

We talked about it over wine and biscuits in George's study.

"It must have been the thunder," said George. "Did you notice how it drowned out the sound of Martin's voice here? At times I could hardly hear what he was saying. The thunder must have disrupted the vibrational pattern just enough to render the incantation useless." He seemed to cheer up as he thought about it. "Of course! That must be the explanation!"

"There is another," said Martin slowly. He licked his thin lips with a nervous gesture and reached for his wine. He seemed a little shrunken, as a man might look who had undergone some tremendous physical exertion, and he drank the rich fluid as though it meant life itself.

"Another explanation?" George was interested. "What is it?"

"It may be that belief in the success of the incantation is essential for its success," said Martin. "The very mental doubt may have just the effect expected, a failure. Can you understand what I am trying to say?"

"Yes," I said, and looked at him. "You mean that I, because of my scepticism, nullified the experiment."

"Exactly." Martin sipped again at his wine. "Oh, don't think that I am throwing the blame wholly on you. I too may be at fault. It could be that a little change of inflection…" He shrugged, and looked at George. "I'm sorry, but we must be realists. No one can really say how the old Latin should sound. I have my theories but I could be wrong. I am sorry, but that is how it is."

"Practice," said George, and slammed his hand down onto his knee. "We all need practice. You, John, to get rid of your doubts. You, Martin, to brush up on the speed of the incantations. Myself, to iron out the little hesitations and gaps in ritual." He chuckled. "No wonder we failed. How could we hope for success at the very first experiment? We must practice, all of us. Practice and practice until we are word and deed perfect. That is the only way we can ever hope for success."

And so we practiced.

I doubt if ever men gave themselves so wholeheartedly to an aim so odd. George had decided to waste no more time and, perhaps because of his previous experiences, or perhaps that, like me, he believed in going to the source of power, the plans were now changed to call up, not a minor demon, but Satan himself.

He made changes in the ritual too.

Night was essential but lack of light was sufficient and so, when we again gathered in the big room, it was well before midnight and the streets outside were busy with people returning home from their evening pleasures. Drums too had been added, a soft, subtle, blood-stirring rhythm culled from old parchments and recorded on a tape recorder for the playback.

Other things had been changed and, when we took up our positions, it was not as three hopeful amateurs playing at wizards, but as three determined men intent heart and soul on calling up the powers of darkness.

George drew the pentagram, the five pointed star with two angles ascendant and the other pointed down. He bathed the points with blood from a canister, then set the five fat candles above the crimson points. The cabalistic symbols followed and then the outer ring of protection. Rising from his stooped position he crossed to the brazier and flung powders onto the glowing charcoal. The fires flared upward, red and green and ghastly yellow. Red tongues rose from the candles and the scent of burning incense caught my throat. I stepped forward and made the ritual gestures to the four points of the compass, to the zenith and nadir, and burned an offering of flesh and wine to the elemental spirits of earth, air, fire and water. I stepped back and took my place by the table as George, lifting his arms, spoke in rolling Latin the preliminary summons of command. As he finished I stooped and switched on the tape recorder and, as the sibilant mutter of drums echoed through the room, Martin stepped forward and, lifting his arms, began the incantation to summon the Devil.

I thought that his thin mouth was a scarlet gash spouting corruption. The words were Latin but the intonation was as the croaking of spawn from the floor of Hell. It rose with a twisted thunder of gutturals and sibilants and, mingled with it, the ceaseless pounding of the drums merged with and amplified the sound. It was just that, sound, but it was redolent with evil and primitive fears.

I felt it. I knew it, even as I wondered at the strange combination of modern and ancient represented by the tape recorder and the old incantation, I felt the hairs at the back of my neck bristle and the sweat bead my forehead with anticipation of what was to come. For now I had no doubt, no scepticism. I knew what we were doing and I knew what the incantation meant.

It was a call straight to Hell.

It was a summons to the Devil.

The drone mingled with the darkness and the darkness mingled oddly with the red tips of the candles and the leaping glow from the brazier. The pentagram became a wriggling serpent, ghastly blue in its phosphorescence, and the surrounding symbols seemed to move and shift with a life of their own. The shadows moved, the drums pounded, the thundering tones of the incantation grew louder and louder until they seemed to almost burst my skull. My eyes dimmed and strange odours assailed my nostrils.

Suddenly the pulsing began.

It shook the walls. It shook the house. It seemed to vibrate every atom in my body. It took the words of the incantation and blended with them, then emerged stronger, triumphant with added power. Smoke swirled from the brazier twisting then, as a great wind filled the room, changing into the squat and horrible shape of something that was not quite human.

Time seemed to halt, to stop so that I hung suspended on the edge of eternity then, with a blasting combination of sound and elemental forces, the pentagram dissolved into wriggling flecks of coloured light and a terrible weight crushed me down to the floor.

"John!"

Someone was shaking me. I opened my eyes and stared up at the worried features of George. I blinked at him and then at the lights.

"What happened?"

"Nothing." He sounded bitter. "You collapsed a moment ago and I put on the lights."

"But I felt something," I protested. "George! There was something in this room, a presence. I'm sure of it."

"Sheer self-hypnosis. The drumming, the lights, the incantation. You expected something to happen and so, to you, it did. But we've failed again." His thin shoulders slumped in utter dejection. "We've failed."

"No," I said, and even to me my voice sounded strange. "We haven't failed. Look!"

I pointed and, as George followed my gesture, I heard the sharp intake of his breath.

"Martin! What are you doing inside the pentagram?"

He asked the question but he knew the answer even as I did. The thing standing within the five-pointed star was not Martin. He looked the same, wore the same clothes, even his smile was the same, but his eyes belonged to nothing human. He looked at us and I shivered at the naked hate in those red eyes. He stepped forward to the edge of the pentagram, then halted as he stared at us. I shivered and fought the desire to run and keep on running away from the thing we had summoned. The thin lines of the pentagram seemed a slender defence against the forces of evil, which we had summoned into this prosaic room in a prosaic house.

"We summoned the Devil," I said, and my voice rose until it hovered on the brink of hysteria. "We called him and he came. But we never thought of what shape he would wear. George! In the old days didn't they use to provide a goat or something for him to enter into?"

"Yes." George sounded as sick and as ill as I did. "I thought that was just a part of the superstition and unnecessary for our purpose. I thought the animal was merely to provide the blood. John! What a fool I've been."

"Steady!" I gripped his shoulders and slapped his face, hard. He calmed, and, avoiding the stare of the thing we had trapped, spoke in quieter tones;

"The explanation is simple. The person uttering the incantation attracts the powers directly to himself via the focus of the pentagram. In the old days, as you reminded me, they used to tie a goat in that focus, cut its throat and let its blood spill onto the ground. Obviously, the spirits, demons, Satan himself, can have no corporeal body such as we know it. It, they, must be an elemental web of force able to enter into and take possession of any other material body."

He swallowed and wiped at his streaming features.

"The sacrificial victim served as a vehicle for the demon. It occupied it until it died and then had to return to its own world. But we neglected to provide such a vehicle."

"It jumped the gap," I said dully, "Like an electrical spark it jumped the gap from the focus to the nearest suitable body. That was Martin. In some way it dragged Martin into the pentagram and there took possession of his body." I stared at George. "But Martin isn't dying. How long will Satan inhabit his body? *And how can we get rid of him?*"

The next few days were a nightmare. We had locked Martin into the room because, as George pointed out, no matter what powers Satan might have had in his free state, yet once in possession of a body he was limited by that body. A solid body cannot walk through walls even though it could cross the lines of the pentagram, and so we locked the room and settled down to a long and serious search for some way to get rid of our visitation.

Strangely enough, neither of us had any desire to ask for all the things we had thought of before the experiment. We still intended to make our demands but now, the important thing was to discover a way in which to control Satan and send him back to his own world. We culled information from mouldering tomes and tattered volumes. I added the fruit of my own labours and we assembled our armoury ready for the test of strength. As yet we had given Martin nothing in the way of food and only a little water. As George explained:

"The weaker he is physically the better chance we shall have of ridding him of his possessor. We can always nurse him back to strength afterwards."

So we starved Martin in the hope that, by so doing, we would also weaken the thing that had taken possession of his body.

Our own armoury consisted of everything said or rumoured to be of avail against the demons of darkness. Holy Water and the Crucifix. Cold iron and silver. I had a knife inscribed with sacred runes from Scandinavia and I added it, together with a revolver loaded with silver bullets and an amulet said to contain a hair from the beard of Mohammed. George shook his head as he looked at them.

"Material weapons can only hurt the material body," he pointed out. "Those silver bullets could kill Martin and rob the Devil of his home, but we must avoid murder."

"It wouldn't be murder." I slipped the pistol in my pocket. "Anything is justified if it means sending Satan back to his own place. Can you imagine what would happen if Martin escaped?"

"I've thought about it," said George, and shuddered. He looked drawn and prematurely old, and I knew the weight he must have on his mind. He looked at me. "John, I want you to let me enter that room alone. There is something I must discover and it might be dangerous." He rested his hand on my knee. "Please. John. Promise me that you will not interfere."

I argued but he was insistent and in the end I had to let him go. I unlocked the door and he entered the room and, locking the door after him, I rested my ear against the panel and tried to follow what was going on inside.

I wish that I hadn't.

There were two voices, one easily recognisable as belonging to George, the other like nothing I had ever heard or dreamed of in my entire life. It was not human. It was as if an ape were chattering through the mouth of a man or, rather, as if something were trying to force human vocal chords to make sounds they were never designed to make. It slobbered did that voice, drooled, made horrible sucking noises and then, towards the last, became clear and strong as though the thing inhabiting Martin's body had finally mastered its new possession.

I sweated as I listened and my hand, as it gripped the butt of my pistol, ached from the strain. I wanted to rip open the door and send my silver bullets crashing into the owner of that vile voice. Only my promise to George and the knowledge that, if I did, I would be murdering the body of an innocent man, restrained me.

What they said in that room I shall never know. George was inside for a long, long time, and once I heard the sound of drumming and twice I caught a whiff of incense. Ugly sounds mingled with the echoes of chanting and there was the sound of threshing and movement unnatural for only two people.

When George finally came out of the room he was pale but his eyes glowed with a new enthusiasm.

I followed him up to his study and stared at him.

"Well?"

"I'm going to feed Martin," he said. "He's terribly weak and I promised that I would look after him."

"You promised?" I stared hard at him and something in his expression awoke new fears within me. "George! What happened in there?"

"Nothing." He avoided my eyes. "We were successful, John, that's all. We did manage to summon Satan and he's trapped in Martin's body." He hesitated. "He spoke to me. There are certain signs known only to the initiate and some gestures…" He broke off and when he looked at me again he was defiant. "Well, we wanted to summon him and we did. I don't know how you feel but I don't think this opportunity should be wasted. Satan promised, things…" His voice faded into silence again and I felt sick with doubt as I stared at my friend.

Rumours came back to me. The ugly one of George's association with the Satanists of Devil Worshippers. He had been mixed up with them to a greater extent than I knew and now that he was confronted by the actual thing he had once worshipped! I took a deep breath Satan was motonous from his promises and he had obviously won George over to his side. I attempted to be casual.

"Did you discover any way to send him back?"

"No. There are chants, I suppose, but we needn't worry about them now." A fire glowed in his eyes as he looked at me. Think of it. John! With Satan to advise and help us we can do great things in the world. Money, power, position, the respect of others. I tell you that there is no limit to what we can achieve. John. We are standing at the threshold of a new life!"

It sounded good. It sounded too good and, even while I warmed to his enthusiasm. I was looking for the catch Satan never gave something for nothing and I remembered Fred's warning and the fate of Sam who had finished up in a lunatic asylum hopelessly insane.

"It sounds wonderful," I said cautiously. "But what do we have to do for all this?"

"Nothing."

"Nothing?"

"Well, almost nothing," he said impatiently. "Martin is weak and naturally Satan wants a new vehicle. We can find him one, someone young and strong, and we can make the transfer by repeating the correct incantation and making the appropriate rituals. Satan will advise us there. Then, after the transfer, we can contact those who will only be too pleased to learn of his coming. We shall form ourselves into a strong party, gain the support of the wealthy and influential, and, before long, we shall have taken over the government of this country."

His eyes sparkled as he looked at me.

"I was right about the alternative path to knowledge, John. With the appropriate sacrifices and rituals it is possible to perform literal miracles. And there is more, much more. Satan has promised to teach me the secrets of body-transference so that, in effect, we shall be immortal. When we grow old we merely change these bodies for new ones. Think of it, John! Think of it!"

I thought of it and the more I thought of it the less I liked it. George was obviously insane. The wild promises he had heard from the thing occupying Martin's body had dazzled his reason. He no longer thought of the evil and hate, the murders and crime that would follow his so-called plan. Satan was evil and no promise he could make would be other than a tempting bribe to gain his own ends. My senses sickened as I thought of what his casual references to sacrifices and body-stealing meant. And there was another side to be considered.

We had opened a door between the worlds of material and demonic things and Satan had come through. Satan was indestructible. We could send him back but we could never destroy him and, as I thought about it, I began to have my first doubts as to whether we could send him back at all.

"Did you break the pentagram, George?" I stared at him as I asked the question and I read my answer in his eyes. "Why?"

"Why not?" He shrugged and attempted a laugh. "Now that we are going to co-operate with him there was no reason to keep him locked within the pentagram. Anyway, I don't think that it would have restrained him. The longer he stays on our plane the stronger he gets and I didn't want to antagonise him."

"I see." I didn't tell him of my secret thoughts. Of my great fear that others would follow where Satan had led. Satan was not the only demon, merely the leader of them. Hell was filled with malignant shapes and entities and, was it not possible that they too would be eager to crowd through the opened door to acquire human bodies and to use the earth as their plaything? But it was no use telling all this to George.

I made him promise not to talk with Satan again until I returned and, on the lying excuse that I was going to search for a new vehicle for Satan, I left the house. I did not look for some unfortunate to act as a host for the thing we had called from the nether regions. Instead I went to a place I had not taken much interest in for too long.

I went to church.

The priest was intelligent, imaginative, and listened to me without interruption. I hid nothing and spoke the truth as I knew it. I did not try to justify myself nor excuse myself but made frank and open confession of what we had done. After I had finished he sat silent for a long time and then, when I had about given up hope, he nodded as if reaching a sudden decision.

"You were wise, my son, to tell me of this. For many years now the Church has fought the powers of darkness and it has not forgotten how best to subdue the evil forces. At what time shall I attend the house?"

I gave him a time, early dark, and left the church with lightened heart and freshened hope. Ridiculous? No. I had meddled in powers as old as time and needed advice and help of experts. Mother Church had fought and vanquished Satan before. I prayed that she would be able to do so again.

I knew that George had broken his promise as soon as I entered the house.

The place stank of incense and reeked of foul odours. A mumbling came from the big room, a droning and hellish chanting and the air was strained as though by tremendous forces. Softly I crept to the door and tested it. It was locked but I had a duplicate key. I did not open it but busied myself for the struggle which was to come.

I checked my revolver and slipped it into my pocket. I arranged strands of wolfbane at wrists and ankles and hung garlic around my neck. I hung the amulet around my throat and carried the rune-inscribed dagger in my left hand. The priest came just as I was finishing my preparations.

He did not deride what I had done but, after listening at the door, silently handed me a crucifix to hang over my shoulders and, uttering a prayer in rapid Latin, touched my eyes, ears, mouth and hands with Holy Water. He took his vestments from a small bag, donned his own crucifix and, with his missal in his hands, nodded to me to open the door.

We looked in at a scene direct from Hell.

George was prostrate on the polished floor and the parquet was red and sticky with blood. Flames guttered from foul-smelling candles and the thing that inhabited Martin's body was sitting on a raised chair as if it were a throne. The tape recorder was on and the air was filled with the mutter of drums and the brazier, red and lambent, filled the air with twisting tendrils of writhing smoke.

I turned off the tape recorder and switched on the lights. I quenched the brazier and kicked out the candles. Martin, or the thing which was inside of him, leapt to its feet and, from its mouth, came a horrible croaking as if it were spitting a curse.

It was answered from the comers of the room and smoke-shapes, squat and horrible, toad-like and amorphous, came hopping towards us. In the ceiling the lights dimmed as though their power was being drained away and fear, such fear as I have never known, clogged my heart and drenched me in perspiration.

I thought that we were lost. I could not conceive of any power able to beat back those legions from hell. I shrank and, within me, my soul shrivelled as if at the touch of searing flame. Satan croaked again, triumphantly, horribly, and the shapes hopped nearer.

They recoiled as the priest began to speak sonorous Latin.

I could follow it, not all, but some, and I knew that, like Martin, the priest was speaking in vibrations rather than words. But the difference was more than that. It was as light compared to darkness, white to black, cleanliness to filth. Strong and powerful the vibrations from the Sonorous Latin filled the room with the age-old rite of exorcism and, as they felt the power of goodness flooding from the servant of God, the things from Hell quivered and shrank as though a great wind had torn away their smoke-bodies.

The lights brightened and the air cleared and only Satan himself and George, still prostrate on the floor, faced the priest.

He advanced towards the thing on the throne, one hand outstretched and his voice rose as it gained commanding power.

"In the name of the Father, the Son and the Holy Ghost…"

The most potent command the world has ever known and one, which when uttered by the correct person, no force of evil could withstand.

Satan screamed!

He threshed, his eyes red pits of fury, his borrowed body writhing as he sought to fight back with all the power at his command. But he was losing and he knew it. Later; if George's plans had materialised, no ritual exorcism would have prevailed against him, but now, alone and helpless, he could do nothing to withstand the thundering command.

And then he was gone.

I felt it and the priest felt it and, to me, it was incredible that the whole world did not feel it. It was as if a cloud had passed from across the face of the sun. As if a heavy weight had been lifted from my soul and sweetness and light had been admitted to a dark and long-locked room.

For a moment Martin stood as he had during the final moments and then, falling as a tree would fall, he toppled and fell.

I caught him before he struck the floor but, even as I cradled him in my arms, I knew that Satan had taken his toll. He had taken it from George too, that poor fool who had dabbled in things too great for human understanding. I rested Martin on the floor and looked at my friend.

He stared back at me with empty eyes, his mouth drooling a little, his fingers tracing idle patterns on the; floor. Like Martin his eyes were as empty as the windows of a deserted house and, like the other man, he had lost all claim to being called human.

Satan had gone, but he had taken his price with him.

Call it the soul, or the mind, or the reason. Call it what you like but I know one thing for certain. Somewhere across the thin veil which divides us from the nether regions both

George and Martin writhe in eternal torment. Their bodies may die but they themselves can never die.

It is that thought which has made me old before my time and causes me to wake screaming during the night.

Because, I too, am not wholly free of blame.

THE HONEST PHILOSOPHER

The trouble with the world is that people are greedy. No one is ever satisfied or, at least, the few that are aren't large enough to count. Take a man who is starving. That man will swear that all he wants to make him contented is three square meals a day. So you fix it that he gets his three squares, find him a job in a diner, maybe, clearing the dishes or washing up, and then what happens?

At first he'll be satisfied, but only until he's filled his stomach. Then he starts getting greedy. He'll want a new suit, some place to live, money for cigarettes, a car and a girl. So he gets them, and then he wants more. More to eat, more to wear, more girls to run around with. Maybe he'll get married and buy a house and raise a bunch of kids, but even then he won't be satisfied. He'll want a glamour puss, maybe a couple, a swank apartment, liquor, stuff like that, and he'll still be wanting something the day he dies. And that was the man, remember, who swore that he'd be happy if he could only get something to eat. It takes a real man to be content, and he can only be that if he knows just what he wants. I know what I want, and I've got it, too, which is more than most people can say. But most people aren't honest, or they aren't philosophers. I'm both.

And there's only one thing an honest philosopher can be.

* * * *

The fire wasn't drawing too good, the corn stalks held too much sap and the pot wasn't what it should be. Beat-up gas cans never make good cooking pots. They wear thin and buckle, and it's no fun trying to keep them balanced on a couple of bricks. It's even less fun when, the wind is blowing and the air damp with recent rain. I blew into the fire, coughed as smoke billowed about me, and made a grab at the pot just as it threatened to topple over. Sammy waited until I had finished what I had to say.

"You curse real fine, doc," he said admiringly. "I guess it must be the book-learning."

"It helps." I sucked at a singed thumb. "What we need is a decent cooking pot."

"I'll get one." Sammy may have looked uncivilized, but his heart was in the right place. "I'll go looking for one right away."

"A big one, mind." Sammy's heart may have been in the right place, but I had some doubts as to his brains. Two centuries ago he would have been called a "natural" and treated with tolerance. Now he was called a "nut" and no one treated him at all. But he could usually follow me if I kept things simple. "A good, solid one, something that will last. And don't steal it."

"Steal what?" Lizard sat up from where he'd been sleeping off the effects of some brew he'd found. He blinked and ran his tongue over his lips. The tongue, together with the dermatitis which had hardened and scaled his skin, made him look more reptilian than usual. The eyes didn't help either. "What you getting Sammy to do?"

"We need a new cooking pot." I nodded to Sammy to send him on his way. Lizard wasn't usually in the best of moods when he woke, and I didn't want him causing trouble. He grunted as he climbed to his feet and grunted again as he squatted cautiously beside the fire. He wasn't cautious enough. He gave a yelp as his left buttock touched the ground and cursed with more vehemence than artistry.

"That lousy, goddam farmer!" He eased himself on the dirt. "You sure you got it all out, Doc?"

"I'm sure."

"It don't feel like it." Lizard winced as he tried to get comfortable. "That yokel must have loaded his scatter gun with broken glass." He swore again. "How about taking another look, Doc?"

It was inevitable that when I took up my new way of life I should be called either "Doc" or "Prof" and of the two I prefer the one I landed with. It has a certain air of dignity, but the side effects are apt to be troublesome. Too many of my colleagues think that I am a real doctor, probably one struck off the register for unethical conduct, and some of the propositions I've had put to me would surprise you.

"Well, Doc?" Lizard was getting impatient. "You going to take a look?"

"No." I was firm. Examining Lizard's bare backside for shot was something I had no intention of doing for the second time. Once had been more than enough. "There's nothing there," I said. "I got it all out when you came staggering back from that chicken hunt. Prodding about now will only make it worse."

He grunted but accepted my professional opinion. His nose wrinkled as he smelt the stew.

"What's to eat?"

"Stew."

"What's in it?" He peered into the can and lifted out something dark and almost shapeless. "What's this? A cat?"

"An owl."

"You sure?" He sniffed, suspicious. "Don't look much like a bird to me."

"You want to take over the cooking?" It was a threat which always worked. Lizard dropped back the corpse and shook his head.

"Hell, no, Doc. You make a fine cook. It's just that with all them funny ideas of yours we could be eating rats and stuff like that." He sniffed again. "Cats I can stomach, owls, too, but I draw the line at rats."

"Nothing wrong with a nice rat." I gave the mixture a stir. "Mice make good eating, too, if you can get enough of them. And snakes; they taste tender, just like chicken. Then there's grasshoppers; you can eat those, too, and snails, and frogs, and…"

"All right, Doc." Lizard was curt. "You don't have to go into detail."

"I was just trying to point out that food is food," I said. "If you'd only look upon your body as a machine and food as fuel, Lizard, then you'd realise that a man has to try real hard before he can die of starvation."

"So you've told me," he said. "Often. It still don't make that slop taste nice."

I didn't bother to answer that one.

People are funny. Lizard, for instance. He was a natural-born hobo, a man who detested work in any shape or form, and was honest enough to admit it. But, like everyone else, he was greedy. He wanted the fine things of life, snazzy clothes, soft cooking, a warm bed at night and a roof over his head. He wanted those things real bad, not bad enough to work for them, but he wanted them in the worst possible way. While we waited for the stew to cook I tried to show him just how wrong he was.

"Money is a curse, Lizard," I said. "When you've got nothing, then you've got nothing to worry about. Start getting possessions and then you start getting trouble. You want trouble?"

"You kidding?" He knew I wasn't. "Money might not make me happy," he said, "but it sure would allow me to be miserable in comfort."

"Maybe." I leaned back and looked at the sky. The wind had driven away the clouds, and the sun had broken through. It was late summer and the air was still warm and comfortable. Soon it would be winter, but that didn't worry me. Come the ice and snow and I'd be way down south where the sun was still shining. It made me feel good to know that I could go where I liked, when I liked, how I liked.

"Look at us," said Lizard. "Three tramps. Maybe it's all right for Sammy, he don't know no better, but how you stick it beats me. You ain't ignorant; the Judge said that the last time the cops picked us up. You could get and hold a job if you wanted."

"I had a job once." I smiled up at the sky. "I had a car, and a house, and all the stuff you long for. I had money in the bank and the finest collection of ulcers ever owned by one stomach. It got so that I couldn't eat, couldn't sleep and was losing my hair. But I was a success—or so everyone kept telling me."

"Yeah?" Lizard didn't believe me.

"I was a business man and, brother, if you want worry, then you be a business man. Trade gets bad and you worry, trade gets good and you worry some more. Worry and business are two sides, of the same coin; you have one and you get the other for free."

"But you lived easy." Lizard dug into his pocket and produced a crumpled butt. He lit it from the fire and breathed smoke. "You had all you wanted."

"No one gets what they want," I corrected. "Not unless they really know what they want. The rest get what they think they want." I relaxed still more. "I passed out one day, Lizard, bum ticker so the doctors told me, and for the first time in years I took time out to think. I did some real hard thinking while I waited, not knowing if I was going to pull out of it or not, and I surprised myself."

Lizard inhaled, not answering.

"You know, Lizard, the only way for a man to be free is not to want anything. As soon as you want something then you put yourself in the power of those who can give it to you."

"Bunk," said Lizard.

"You think so?" I rolled over, resting on one arm, staring at him. "You want to smoke, right?"

"Sure."

"You bum butts or you buy tobacco. To buy it you have to get someone to agree to give you money. To do that you've got to do as he says. Right?"

"You could look at it that way." Lizard was reluctant to agree. "But when I've got the money for the butts, what then?"

"Then you can be free again—only you won't." I rolled back to my original position. The sky was a lot more pleasant to look at than Lizard's face. "Smoking is a habit. Nice clothes are a habit. Eating off plates and drinking out of glasses, sleeping in beds and reading papers, all habits. And you pay for acquiring those habits, Lizard. You pay and keep on paying." I took a deep breath. "Me, I got no habits."

"The old tune," he sneered. "Next you'll be telling me that only you and those like you are really free."

"It's the simple truth. I don't want anything, so no one can take what I want. I can't lose anything so no one has any power over me. They can jail me, sure, but so what? I don't want to go anywhere particular, do anything special. I can sleep in a cell as easy as on the ground."

"That's what you told the Judge," reminded Lizard. "He thought you was crazy. Hell, I think you're crazy."

Sammy came back just then and interrupted my reply.

He didn't return alone. He had a pot for company, a battered thing of brass, green with verdigris and knocked almost shapeless. I recognised it though; it had once been a spittoon. Sammy explained how he'd got it while Lizard dished up the stew.

"Man at the saloon threw it out." He chewed and spat out a bone. "Will it do?"

"You ain't figuring to cook in that thing." Lizard stared his disgust. "It'll kill us."

"We'll clean it first," I assured. "It looks solid and should do." I put the thing aside while I concentrated on my food. That was another lesson I kept trying to teach to others. Food is meant to be eaten, to be chewed, tasted, savoured and swallowed. That way you enjoy it, your stomach can handle it and you get the full benefit. Gulping it down as if you're in a race is a sure-fire way to collect ulcers.

After the meal I gave some attention to the pot. It was old and had probably been collecting dust for half a century. It was logical that it should have been thrown out, but I had to make sure.

"Did you steal it?"

"No." Sammy looked straight at me. "Honest, Doc, the man gave it to me for free."

I believed him and so did Lizard.

"Who'd want to hold onto a thing like that?" he said. "It's just junk."

"It'll make a good pot." I rubbed at it and was rewarded by the gleam of brass. The metal had a pattern and I could imagine it back in the old days when such things had been used. "Once we get it polished up with sand it'll look real good."

"What about the inside?" Lizard didn't seem too happy. "You're aiming for us to eat out of that thing remember?"

"We'll clean that, too." I handed it to Sammy. "Here, you do it. Use sand and water and plenty of elbow grease. Lizard can take over when you've had enough."

"With my sore leg?" Lizard scowled but hunched forward to watch as Sammy got to work. Half-wit or not, he was willing, and sweat shone on his face as he scrubbed and rubbed at the pot. He finished the outside and started on the interior, using plenty of sand and water as he rubbed away the accumulated grime. He hummed to himself as he worked, an odd, wordless tune he'd probably picked up from some juke box and almost forgotten. It was while he was humming and scrubbing that it happened.

There was a gush of smoke, a tingling sensation like a mild electric shock and a peculiar scent of must and decay. A voice rumbled through the air and a great face glared down at us from the cloud of smoke.

"Hell!" Lizard forgot his lacerated rump as he scrabbled away. "It's a bomb!"

Sammy said nothng, just sat, open-mouthed as he stared at the apparition. It writhed, coalesced and became an old man with a dirty white turban and a knee-length frock coat. He reminded me of a palmist I'd once met, and there was a good reason for him looking so old and tired. He was old, about five thousand years old if I'd guessed right, and anyone would get tired in that time.

"Hail, master," he said wearily. "I am yours to command."

He sat cross-legged on the ground and stared at Sammy with a patient expression.

"I don't believe it!" Lizard was emphatic. "That stuff's for the birds."

"All right, give me a better explanation." I pointed to the pot where it lay, glistening in the dying rays of the sun.

"Sammy rubs the pot and the Jinn appears. What more do you want?"

"Gin?" Lizard scowled. "That guy wasn't no gin."

"Jinn." I spelt it for him. "Aladdin's Lamp. Get it?"

"Where did he go?" Sammy was worried. After the initial appearance I'd ordered the Jinn to leave us and await our call. He hadn't obeyed. Only Sammy, it seemed, had the right power. Sammy'd backed me, but was now worrying about the disappearance of the stranger.

"He'll be back," I said. "Just rub the pot and he'll be back."

"I don't get it," said Lizard. "That pot must have been polished lots of times in the past. Why now?"

"I don't know. Try it again, Sammy."

"Will it be all right, Doc?"

"Sure, try it again." I watched as Sammy rubbed. He began to sweat and nothing happened. Lizard snorted.

"See?"

"Try some other place." I remembered something. "And sing, you know, that song you were humming. Start humming and rub the same place where you was rubbing before."

It took a long time and I was beginning to get worried when finally Sammy managed to hit the right combination. The gush of smoke came again, together with the mild shock and the rest of it. I stared at the old man standing before us."

"Are you a Jinn?" He glanced at Sammy, who nodded. "Go ahead and talk to Doc."

"As you desire, master." The old man sighed. "I am, indeed, the Slave of the Lamp, imprisoned therein by Solomon and constrained to obey those who command."

"Nuts!" Lizard was getting annoyed. "This thing ain't a lamp, it's a goddam spittoon."

"The metal in which my essence was imprisoned has undergone many changes," said the Jinn tiredly. "I had hopes..." He shrugged.

"Hopes that you would be free from the commands of your masters?"

"Even so." He glanced towards me and I could guess just how he felt. For me one lifetime having to do as others wanted had been half a lifetime too much. I felt sorry for the old guy. Sammy sensed it, too.

"You ain't no slave," he said. "You don't have to be kicked around."

"You release me?" The flame of hope in the Jinn's eyes was something to see. I felt proud as I looked at Sammy. It's always heartening to any philosopher to see the fruits of his teaching.

"Sure," said Sammy. "You don't owe me nothing."

"The blessings of Allah be upon you and yours to the end of time!" The Jinn seemed to shed his age like a snake its skin. "May your..."

"Hold it!" Lizard had been thinking. "You can't do that, Sammy."

"Why not?" Lizard waved me to silence.

"We're partners, ain't we? What we got we share, right?" He didn't wait for an answer. "Well, I figure I got a share in this thing and I aim to collect." He sucked in his cheeks. "Now, if I get it right, this old guy will do whatever Sammy tells him to do."

"So?"

"So, before Sammy turns him loose, I reckon that he ought to do something for us." He became cunning. "It's only fair, ain't it?"

"I guess so." Sammy was troubled. "Is that right, Doc?"

"Greed," I said. "Everyone's the..." The Jinn cut me short.

"My gracious master has already released me from bondage," he said. "Yet I would not cause dissension. This I will do. To each of you I will be servant to the extent of one command. What you desire you shall have." He folded his arms over his chest. "I have spoken."

He'd said enough.

What would you say if you had the chance of making a wish that would come true? And you'd have to answer straight away, remember; no chance for talking it over with friends and studying the market. The Jinn was raring to go, and we had to make it fast. Personally, I didn't have to think, I knew what I wanted. Sammy, too. I'd taught him well, or I thought I had, and he spoke up without hesitation. Lizard's choice was obvious.

"Money," he said. "I want money."

"Ten sacks of dinars will I bring," promised the Jinn. "Ten sacks of well-tanned hide filled to the brim." I yelled for him to stop, just in time.

"What's wrong?" Lizard was impatient to get his hands on the money.

"Dinars are made of brass," I explained. "Legal tender in his time, but scrap metal now. Think again."

"Sure." Lizard was shaken. "Gold?"

"Currency regulations; you need a licence to own gold."

"It's heavy, too." Lizard frowned in thought. "A diamond," he said. "The biggest damn diamond in the world." He grinned at me as the Jinn vanished. "Smart, eh? Portable currency, good anywhere." His grin vanished as the Jinn reappeared and put something before him. "Is that a diamond?"

It was as big as a football and looked like a stone. I prodded it, turned it and shrugged.

"It's a diamond, all right. An uncut one; you didn't specify that it should be polished, remember."

"But it's valuable?"

"It's the biggest in the world."

"That's all I want to know." Lizard may have had a sore leg, but he forgot it as he scooped up the stone and ran towards the village. I watched him go, feeling a little sorry for him. He'd be robbed or murdered for sure, either that or spend the rest of his life in jail trying to explain how he got the rock in the first place.

"Well?" With Lizard gone the Jinn was a little less impatient.

"You know what I want," I said. "I just want to be left alone."

"Nothing else?" The Jinn seemed surprised. "No gold, no jewels, no fair women, mansions, palaces, rich foods, heady wines, soft music? Nothing?"

"Nothing." I thought of something. "Don't get me wrong about this. I don't want people to avoid me or be prevented from helping me. It's just that I'm an honest philosopher. I've worked out my own way of life and I want to stick to it. I don't want anyone bothering me. I just want to be left alone."

"I hear and obey." The Jinn bowed and looked at Sammy. "And for you, master?"

Sammy told him what he wanted.

"I want to be happy," he said. "Happy all the time."

"Happy, master?" The Jinn seemed disconcerted.

"He knows the real values in life," I said. "Sammy's like me, a philosopher."

"That's right." Sammy grinned. "All I want is to be happy."

"All?" The Jinn cast up his eyesr "Think well, master. Much can I give you, soft maidens to while away your cares, pleasant…"

"I don't want nothing to while away no cares," said Sammy. "I don't want no cares to while away. I just want to be happy."

"Truly happy, master?"

"Sure. Happy all the way."

"It shall be as you desire," said the Jinn quietly. "Master, farewell!"

There was a puff of smoke, a crackling sound and a flash of light. When I could use my eyes again I found that I was alone.

Really alone. Lizard had gone, the pot had gone, the Jinn had gone, and Sammy…

Where he had sat was a charred and empty space, and, looking at it, I cursed myself for a fool.

Any philosopher should have known that a man can only be truly happy when he is dead.

THE DOLMEN

Basil Heather came to the parish of Millhaven with firm ideas about quashing all the country nonsense he was convinced occupied most of the thoughts of his parishioners. A bustling, officious man of medium height and round girth with a glint in his eyes and determination in the set of his jaw, he was of the modern school who believed in nothing that they could not touch or see. Aside from orthodox religion, of course, and even m that he had little patience with those who wished to argue theology.

The parish, however, had been spoiled by Dr. Wenton, Heather's predecessor who had been lenient almost to the point of idiocy, or so Heather thought when he came to look over his new living. Funds that should have been earmarked for a new organ or the restoration of the roof of the small but agreeably old church, had been squandered on Morris Dances and similar stupidity which everyone of intelligence knew to be connected with the old, pre-Roman worship. Indeed, the debt of the parish was such that any other man might well have thrown up his hands and let things ride while waiting for a dispensation from providence or, far more likely, a bequest in the will of some of the local gentry.

However, there he was and in Millhaven he meant to stay.

He was not married but he employed a housekeeper, a gardener and occasionally hired a chauffeur driven car. He took complete possession of the vicarage and in a short while had taken complete possession of the village and its various activities too. These he reorganised with the main object in mind of reducing the debt of the church and laid out a complete programme of whist drives, benefits, amateur theatricals and raffles which would have kept a village three times the size of Millhaven busy for the best part of a year.

Unfortunately, as he soon began to realise, no one, not even the most energetic vicar can obtain blood from a stone or money from those who haven't got it and it was forced upon him that he had to find some other solution to the problem.

Inevitably he thought of the local legend.

About two miles from the village, set on a rolling slope of the downs, was an old dolmen, which had been there ever since the villagers could remember. Indeed, it was said that it had been there before the Romans came and was the burial site of the old chiefs who had fallen in battle. Heather, while not disputing the legend, had his own ideas that were supported by the Squire, bluff Sir Welby of Welby Hall, the local magistrate and the authority on everything in the vicinity. Over a bottle of rare port to which he had been invited Heather mentioned the subject on his mind.

"The Dolmen?" Welby nodded. "Of course I know it. Know all about it too I dare say. Pre-Roman I'd swear to it. Possibly connected up with the old Druids and some of their sacrifices or other tomfoolery. What makes you ask?"

"I've heard that it is a burial mound or community grave of the old chieftains," said Heather thoughtfully. "I'm inclined to believe that is true. In such a case it would be worth excavating the mound to discover whether there are any works of art or weapons or things of intrinsic or historical value there. The old burial customs used to insist that a chief be buried with his jewellery and eating utensils." He sipped at his port. "It would be interesting to excavate the mound to discover its exact date."

"Don't do it," said Welby promptly. "Leave well alone, that's my motto and that's what I always do. We like the Dolmen the way it is, don't want a lot of foreigners coming here to dig it up. Why, it's a landmark for miles around... useful when on the hunt."

To the Squire as to the rest of the villagers anyone not born in the parish was a foreigner. Heather had been uncomfortably aware that he was so classed but, because of his cloth and calling, he had been given a special sort of dispensation as it were so that it was tacitly assumed that he was Millhaven born and bred by adoption if not by fact.

"So you advise against it, Squire?"

"I do," said Welby firmly. "Have some more port."

Heather followed the suggestion but did not take the advice. As he needed the support, both financial and moral of the Squire he did not press the point about excavating the Dolmen but retired to find fresh guns to bear on the old man's prejudices. He found them in the nature of old parchments, which, quite by accident, he found between the leaves of an old missal tucked away in the study. The next time he and the Squire met he was armed with new information.

"About the Dolmen," he said as soon as they were seated. "I've found some papers which gives me reason to believe that certain treasure was buried there at the time of the Dissolution. There used to be a monastery about here, I understand, and they hid much of their plate and vessels to save them from the ministers of King Henry VIII." He carefully folded his parchment. "See? It states quite plainly that certain items were buried at the site of the Dolmen."

"And dug up again later, no doubt," said the Squire. "But I'm glad that you brought that paper with you. I have one of my own in the library and it should interest you."

He rose and, with much muttering and fumbling about, returned with a cracked and sered scrap of paper yellowed with age and brittle with time. Heather took it with the respect he had for anything very old and carefully unfolding it read the crabbed writing which covered it.

"It seems very clear," he said thoughtfully. "In Latin, of course, but that presents no problem. I majored in Latin as one of the subjects of my B.A." The explanation given and the old man suitably impressed he returned to his reading.

"This seems to be an account of a predecessor of yours as to what was supposed to have taken place at the Dolmen about three hundred years ago." He read on, his lips moving as he translated the crabbed writing. "A coven of witches was suspected to assemble there and to perform wild and unnatural rites to the general disturbance of the peace. A raid was made and two men and three women arrested, later tried for witchcraft, and publicly burned at the stake." He looked at the Squire. "Superstition and the account of a clerk with an inflamed imagination."

"Read on," said Welby comfortably. "The last part is more interesting."

Heather read on, slightly embarrassed by his host's own knowledge of the dead language. When he had read to the end he snorted and put down the paper.

"So strange things were supposed to have happened in the disturbers of that Dolmen. After the trial it was decided to destroy the stone and a barrel of gunpowder was used for the purpose. It failed but the explosion injured ten men. A second attempt also failed but this time the crops failed, the cows ran dry, and strange manifestations terrified the village. There was no third attempt and, as far as we know, the Dolmen has been left undisturbed unto this day."

"Correct," said Welby. "And I say that it's best left alone."

Heather sighed and began the hard task of convincing the old man that he was both out of date and hopelessly stupid. It is not surprising that both men began to lose their tempers.

"Say what you wish, Squire, but I intend to excavate that mound. If you refuse to help me then I shall appeal to the village."

"You'll get no help from them," snapped the old man. "They know better than to mess about with things best left alone. You're new here so you wouldn't understand, but I'll take a bet that you won't get a single man to help you."

"I shall shame them into helping me," said Heather firmly. "It isn't as if I want them to actually do anything but obey my orders. Once they shift the stone I can continue with the excavations myself."

Welby brightened and smiled for the first time since the argument had begun.

"That might not be so bad then. As I understand it the curse applies only to the actual disturber of the Dolmen, so you won't be really loosing any trouble on the parish if you take it all on yourself."

"Curse?" Heather sighed. "Not another of those stupid legends."

"You can call it stupid," said Welby darkly. "But I for one wouldn't like to bring it upon myself."

Heather had some difficulty in restraining himself. He reminded the Squire that this was, after all, the twenty-first century and not the dark ages and repeated his determination to have the stone shifted as soon as he could arrange to do so. Shortly after he took his leave and it was not until he was almost home that he remembered that he had neglected to inquire as to the precise nature of the curse. He dismissed it from his mind as being of no possible importance and spent the next few days gathering as much information about the Dolmen as he could.

Two weeks later the work was begun, everyone taking the utmost care so that the great stone should not be damaged in any way. The vicar told himself and others that he was not a vandal. Nevertheless it was a sullen group of men that assembled at the site and began to dig away the dirt from around the edge of the stone. Only his searing remarks from the pulpit and his personal assurance that he would hold himself responsible for any curse or malignant manifestations had persuaded them to agree to do the task at all.

The work was long and arduous and needed plenty of patience. At first Heather had hoped that the local breakdown wagon would be able to lift the stone and swing it to one side with its crane, but, after one glance at the stone, the owner had emphatically stated that the crane big enough to move that weight hadn't yet been mounted on wheels. He did, however, offer the loan of several bars and wedges and promised that, when the dirt had been cleared away, he would see what could be done to topple it over.

Heather himself was full of enthusiasm. Already he could see the big write-ups in the illustrated papers of the wonderful finds he would make and he toyed with the idea of presenting some odd work of art to the British Museum with, naturally, his name attached as donor. Second thoughts however persuaded him that it would be financially better for the village to have its own museum attached to the excavated site. Postcards would be sold and a souvenir booklet of which he had already made a rough draft. The income would be small but surely enough to keep the church once and for all out of debt. His own rewards would automatically come with the preferment his success would deserve.

After two weeks of steady digging the men announced that it would be dangerous to continue and Heather sent for the garage proprietor and warned him to bring his heaviest and strongest breakdown wagon. The warning was unnecessary, the man only had the one, but he arrived at the site shortly after receiving the telephone message and, with himself supplying the knowledge and Heather the unwanted supervision, he readied everything for the toppling over of the stone.

Dirt was scraped away from beneath each end and strong cables passed beneath and around the mass of granite. The wagon was backed and the cables fitted. Men were stationed with bars and wedges to thrust beneath the lifted edge and, when everything was ready, the owner climbed into his vehicle and slowly drove forward.

A shout from the watching men warned that the stone was lifting and they thrust in their wedges. The engine of the wagon roared, dirt plumed from beneath the wheels, and one of the cables parted with the sound of a cracking whip.

That it missed decapitating the vicar was something the villagers never understood. He had stooped at that very moment and, just before he straightened, the broken end of the thick cable lashed the air just above his head. Had it made contact Heather would have lost all interest in matters earthly. Even as it was, pale and shaken at the near escape, he did no more than chide the garage owner for faulty equipment and suggest that perhaps it would be better if some other method was attempted.

The garage owner, without mentioning the cost of the ruined cable, agreed, and rigged up a double-strength chain attached to a grapnel. Warning everyone to stand clear he drove forward again and, as the scene of burning rubber from his spinning tyres filled the twilight, the men yelled encouragement as they thrust home their wedges.

"Good," smiled the vicar proudly as he examined the widening gap. "One more good pull should see the job finished."

He smiled around at the men and promised them all a treat if they would stick at the task. He knew that, once they had a chance to think about it and to consider the story, his near miss would be interpreted as a direct sign of malign powers. As he hoped the prospect of free beer persuaded them to get the job over and done with and, as the engine strained and the men sweated, the great stone slowly toppled from where it had lain for untold centuries into the new bed prepared for it.

The only other damage at that time was the total loss of the chain, which, caught beneath the mass of granite, could not be salvaged.

Beneath the stone was a flat slab of some strange substance resembling slate, which was firmly set into the ground. Heather examined it, quivering with eagerness to discover what was beneath, but it was late and the men were restless and he decided to put off further investigations until the next day. Besides, he would rather examine the treasure, which he was convinced lay beneath the slab without witnesses. Gossip was rife in the village and he had no desire for awkward questions to be asked concerning the fate of some jewelled object of rare worth or other items of a similar nature. The vicar, in everything including his religion, was of an intensely practical turn of mind.

There was a message waiting him when he returned to the vicarage after seeing to the rewarding of his helpers. Sir Welby answered the phone and coughed as Heather introduced himself.

"Just rang to find out whether you were all right, Heather," he said gruffly. "Are you?"

"Of course I'm all right. What makes you think I'm not?"

"Just my curiosity," murmured the Squire. "I heard about that accident you almost had. Rather nasty thing, what?"

"It was an accident," said the vicar sternly. "I am fully aware that gossip will try and make something supernatural out of it, but it was plainly due to a bad cable."

"Of course," said the old man hastily. "Never said it wasn't, still, you never know." He coughed again. "By the way, if you should need me, just give me a ring. I've an extension on my bedside table and I could be with you in ten minutes."

The vicar made short work of that suggestion. When he put down the telephone he was certain that the old Squire must have long passed his prime and be well on the road to senile decay. He also decided to draft out a series of sermons ridiculing superstition and those who should know better than to spread such nonsense. The Squire, while a person of some importance in the community, should learn that times changed and that there was no room for the old village nonsense.

When he finally put out the light and went to bed Heather was busy compiling, mentally at least, the preface to his proposed booklet describing the trouble he had had with local prejudice before he could excavate the site beneath the stone.

He was awakened in the night by what first he thought was the patter of rain against his window pane but, as he came more fully to his senses, he recognised it as a kind of snuffling sound, the kind of sound an animal would make. At the same time he was conscious of a terrific din from the village. It seemed that every dog for miles around was barking with a frenzied madness as if they were frightened or angry at something.

Rising, the vicar crossed to the window and looked out. From his vantage point, his room was on the second storey of the vicarage, he could see most of the village spread out before him. Lights shone in most windows and the harsh voices of men trying to control their dogs increased rather than diminished the noise. It wasn't raining and Heather was at a loss to account for what had made the noise at his window, when he became aware of something staring at him.

He looked up sharply just in time to catch a glimpse of a shadowy shape flit away into the night and, together with its going, the dogs ceased their barking and quieted down. The sudden jangling of the telephone made the vicar jump.

"Is that you, Heather?" said old Welby. "Just thought I'd call to see if everything was all right. Did you hear the noise?"

"Yes, it's died down now." Heather forced himself to remember that the old man meant well. "But it wasn't that which woke me." He described the noises he had heard at the window.

Welby was silent for a long time and when he spoke his words didn't make sense to the vicar, now shivering with the cold and thinking longingly of his warm bed.

"Dogs. They used to bury dogs with the chiefs in the old days. Or ravens? Could it have been ravens?"

Heather slammed down the receiver.

The next day he collected a couple of crowbars, a heavy hammer, a rucksack and a pick and shovel and had the garage owner drop him and his load off at the side of the stone.

There were a few lookers on hanging about, none of them too near, and the vicar had the unpleasant feeling that they were waiting for something to happen to him rather than waiting to see what he was going to do. He ignored them and, scraping away the dirt around the edges of the strange slab, began to lever with the crowbars until he felt something yield.

As it did so there was a terrible crack of thunder from the sky and a wind blew across the downs with such force that it almost blew the vicar's hat from his head.

"Confounded storm coming up," he muttered. "At least it will keep the others away from the site. I wish that I'd remembered to bring a raincoat."

For a moment he hesitated between continuing his excavations or returning to the vicarage for his raincoat. However, that would have meant a five mile walk and consequent loss of time and the vicar was not a patient man. So he redoubled his efforts and finally, after much groaning and reluctance, the slab tilted up, there to be propped by a convenient piece of rock.

Heather looked down into utter darkness.

"Faugh!! He turned his head to avoid the dank, stale odour thar came welling upwards toward him. "This must be the burial chamber. That air must have been trapped down there for two thousand years."

He didn't stop to remember that burial mounds did not have burial chambers as such but were merely dirt and stone piled onto the dead. He didn't think it strange either that the Dolmen wasn't a true dolmen as such but was merely an unsupported slab of granite. More like a weight than anything else and certainly not a religious structure.

He peered into the darkness again and this time ventured to light a match. It went out immediately and so did a second.

"It will take time to let that bad air clear," he said thoughtfully. He glanced up at the sky. "That storm is coming nearer. I wonder if I have time to get home and return before it breaks?"

Another rumble of thunder decided him and, after making quite certain that there was no one about whom he could send on an errand, he decided to tackle the five mile walk. Not, as he told himself, that it would be time wasted. The ninety minutes or so necessary for the double journey would enable the stale air in the vault to be cleared and, as it was so dark down there, he would return with a flashlight. A short examination today to discover any jewelled objects or similar works of like value, and he would invite old Welby for an inspection tomorrow. At least, his find would convince the old man that he knew what he was talking about.

Heather was quite jubilant as he strode across the downs and not even the warning drops of rain pattering on his black hat dampened his enthusiasm.

He had a little trouble finding his torch and there was a message from his bishop and another from a parishioner who had an urgent matter to discuss. These things took time, the parishioner proved unexpectedly difficult, and it was not until a couple of hours had passed that the vicar could make his way back to the site. It was raining by then, cold sheets of penetrating rain, which drove every sensible man indoors and even sent the birds huddling on their branches.

Dressed in his raincoat and filled with curiosity as to what he would find the vicar made light work of the rain. Also, if the truth were known, it wasn't just curiosity which drove him. He was filled with the fear that someone might lower himself down into the vault before he returned and there was no knowing what damage might be done or what items stolen.

The vicar, even though he was a newcomer to the parish, had quite managed to convince himself that the Dolmen and all it contained was his personal property to be used to pay off the church debt, of course, but by himself and none other.

He almost ran the last few hundred yards to the site and when he reached it could have cried out at what he saw.

Someone had closed the slab again.

It must have been deliberate, he distinctly remembered propping it up with a piece of rock, and he felt a sudden fear that someone had emptied the tomb before him. This ungenerous thought was replaced by another as he looked around for the tools he h(ad brought with him. Suppose someone had lowered themselves down into the chamber and the slab had then fallen shut behind them? It was possible, an accidental knock could have dislodged the rock, and, as he remembered, the stone slab was far too heavy to be pushed up from within.

Hastily he looked for a crowbar.

He had trouble finding one. The same malicious person who had shut the slab had, for reasons of his own, scattered the tools far and wide. The vicar had a hard job locating even one of them and when he finally found a crowbar it was in a bush some three hundred yards from where he had left it. He decided to be very firm with the person responsible and, perspiring freely inside his raincoat, he set to work once again on the slab.

This time, when he had managed to lift it, he threw it right over so that it couldn't possibly be closed by accident again. Dropping the crowbar he knelt at the edge of the opening and called down to whoever was inside.

"Hello, there! Are you hurt?"

His voice echoed and rolled and came back to him strangely distorted. He tried again.

"This is Heather, the vicar, can you hear me?"

He waited until the echoes died away then, taking his torch from his pocket, shone it into the opening.

About ten feet below him he saw something white and ghastly familiar. He had attended enough burials to have become inured to the thought of death but there was something about the pitiful heap of bones below which upset him. The emotion lasted but a moment for, as he reminded himself, what else could he have expected in a burial chamber but bones?

He looked again, shining the light about the chamber but aside from the skeleton he saw nothing but a round hole in one side of the vault. Obviously this was merely the ante-chamber or outside vault and the skeleton was that of a slave set to guard the outer portal. So the vicar told himself and gained some comfort from it.

Thunder burst overhead as he stared into the vault and the rain began to come down with redoubled force. For a moment he considered the possibilities of dropping down into the vault and having a look at the treasures, which must undoubtedly lie down the tunnel. He considered it, then reluctantly gave up the idea. Getting down was no problem but the floor was ten feet down and if lowered himself into the chamber he doubted his ability to climb out again.

As no one knew that he was at the site and as it was terrible weather and getting on towards sunset, it was quite possible that, if he trapped himself, he would have to stay there the entire night.

Slowly he straightened and considered what best to do. He could replace the slab, he supposed, and that would keep the chamber dry. It would also discourage whoever it was who had tampered with it before. On the other hand it would waste more time but, as he would need a ladder and other things, he could get the garage owner to come out in his wagon and help him.

The decision made, the vicar levered at the stone until he had manoeuvred it back into its original position. Then, after a last glance around, he began to make his long way home.

He became aware of the presence shortly after he had left the site. It seemed to hover all around him like an evil cloud and, as he walked, he became aware again of the same peculiar snuffling as had wakened him the previous night.

Imperceptibly he lengthened his stride and, at the same time, looked around him for a familiar form. The downs were deserted, the rain filling the air with mist, and he seemed to walk alone in a world of his own.

He had walked a long time before something loomed up before him and, to his surprise, he found that he was back at the site of the disturbed stone.

"Strange," he said. "I must have walked in a circle. It must have been the mist."

It upset him a little but not much for, as everyone knows, it is very easy to walk in a circle if there are no familiar landmarks to steer by. Desert travellers do it all the time and people have often done it when thinking of other matters. So, at least, the vicar told himself but his peace of mind was rudely shattered when, after an hour's walk, he found himself back in the same place once more.

This time he sat down to rest awhile and, as he sat, he became aware of the presence more strongly than before. He shook himself, angry at the thoughts filling his mind and, tired as he was, he set out once more through the rain and the thickening dusk towards the village.

He walked with greater care this time, watching where he was going and trying not to imagine that something was following his every step. It wasn't easy to do that because the snuffling sound had grown louder and joined with it was a peculiar rustling as if something huge and invisible were marching at his side.

Heather glanced towards the sound, narrowing his eyes as he stared at the darkening mist, and vaguely, he thought he could see a monstrous shape walking beside him. It was terrible that shape, so terrible that he forgot his discipline and impatience at the old beliefs and began to run hard towards the safety of the village, to the bright lights at home and to the sound of the old Squire's calm voice.

He ran until his legs ached and he could hardly breathe and then, when he was near to collapse, he felt his foot catch on something and he went sprawling on hands and knees.

Somehow he wasn't surprised to find that he was lying across the slab back at the site of the huge stone.

He sprawled and fought for breath while, all the time, a little primitive part of his mind was screaming a warning to get up and run.

He tried and struggled to his feet. He even took a step away from the stone then, as a great shadow loomed above him, he tilted back his head and screamed at the top of his lungs.

The scream was cut off as though with a knife.

A labourer, wending his tired way home from a hard day in the fields heard the scream and, muttering something under his breath, tucked in his elbows and ran towards the village. Later, after he had fortified himself at the bar of the inn, he went up to see the old Squire and the two of them sat for a long while in talk. Afterwards the labourer denied he had heard anything at all.

The Squire, as soon as the night had passed and it was day, saddled his horse and went for a ride. It was possibly by sheer chance that he rode towards the site of the Dolmen.

It wasn't the same as it had been the day before.

The great stone, moved with so much time and effort, dragged and toppled from its age-old bed, had somehow been replaced.

The Squire looked at it for a long time then, slowly dismounting, he walked towards it and spent a long time examining its base. He kicked a heap of dirt over something he saw and then, his seamed old face serious, he mounted and rode back to the village.

Some men came out afterwards and shovelled dirt back into the place they had taken it from. Some of them even shovelled dirt high around the base of the stone as if they wanted to be certain that every crack and gap was filled. Only when they were satisfied that all was as it had been did they return to the village.

For a while there was talk about the missing vicar but it soon died because no one had really liked him and, as the Squire was also the magistrate, they left it to him to decide what official action, if any, should be taken.

None ever was.

The Squire made a report to the Church Authority and as far as anyone knew, Heather had just run away one day and never returned.

But the Squire spent some time reading an old parchment, a companion to the one Heather had laughed at, and what he read seemed to satisfy him that everything was in order. He would have warned the vicar more than he had done but for the man's laughter and scorn. For what modern man could conceive of a burial vault for something not of this earth? Old powers had trapped it, chained it, and sealed the tomb with a human sacrifice. That same power had resealed the burial vault after the vicar had so unwisely opened it after so many years.

It was only poetic justice that he, in his turn, should have served as the living victim necessary to seal the vault.

They have a new vicar at Millhaven now. He is a simple, quiet old man who spends much of his time in the garden and plays chess with the Squire and a few of his cronies. He doesn't interfere with the village in any way and doesn't worry about the church debt. He has only visited the Dolmen once, and that was after a long talk with the Squire. They went out early one Sunday before anyone was about and what they did didn't take very long.

It was a simple service, not quite the thing Heather would have chosen had he been able, but, as the Squire said, he couldn't possibly grumble about the size of his monument.

He even placed a few wild flowers over the spot where he had seen a shred of black protruding past the stone, a scrap of material it was of the sort of which clerical raincoats are made.

But the Squire was glad he had arranged for the burial service.

He thought that Heather would have appreciated it.

BEWARE!

Beware of the Dealer in Dreams. Beware of the tubby Judas with his round face and twinkling eyes and the eternal good humour of him. Walk gently and tread soft and do not linger to inspect his wares or to satisfy idle curiosity for his words are as honey and his smile is as honest as that of a child, and sure, what harm could there be in such a man at all?

None, if you cannot find him and if you cannot then it's safe enough that you are though perhaps the poorer because of it. Not everyone can have the eyes to see the tiny shop, all squeezed and with the look of falling apart and yet seeming as strong as the rocks of Killorne all at one and the same time. But though it may not be easy to see yet it is as real as the imagination-world of children and as real as the stuff in which the owner deals. As real as the little people and they are real enough as any old wife will tell you and the more fool you for not believing. And if it takes a special kind of person to see the tiny folk then it takes no less to recognise the shop of the Dealer in Dreams.

Such a man was Sean O'Donnell, a tall, gangling man with the smell of peat in this threadbare suit and the kiss of sun and wind marked in freckles on his long-nosed, long-lipped face. A happy man was Sean with never a care as to where he next would sleep or where he would eat if at all. A simple man with the simple faith that things would come if they were to be sent his way and for sure, what was the use of worrying when the sun was shining and there was so much to see in this place? And if he was put out over the lack of gold which was supposed to line the streets and if his throat was raw at the stink of the motors which was a bad thing and an offence to God to so spoil the sweet air, there were compensations for all of that.

One of them passed him so close he could smell the flower-scent of her, a bright-eyed colleen with a figure which caught the breath in his throat and a saucy way of walking which would have earned her hard words from the women and hard looks from Father Rosen had she been back in Ballinasloe. But Sean was no woman and no priest either, God be thanked, so he smiled at her as she passed and let what he felt show in his eye so that her step faltered and a baby dawn rose in her cheeks.

"It's a fine day," said Sean for he was never at a loss for a word when a word was needed. "And sure, it's a finer day because of yourself passing this way, that it is."

"Cheek," said the girl and would have passed on but the Devil had her by the feet so that she hesitated long enough to see the red hair like a field of wind-tossed grain in the sunset and the laughing eyes as blue as the skies over Galway.

"It is not," said Sean. "It is the simple truth that I'm telling. Sure and I've travelled far and never knew until this minute why I was travelling at all." And he smiled again so that she couldn't see the two inches of wrist hanging from the frayed cuffs of his jacket or the broken shoes on his feet so blinded was she by what he had within him.

"Cheek," she said but smiled as she said it, her lips curving as if the Devil himself had taught her the arts of temptation.

"I'll not be asking if I shall be seeing you," said Sean boldly. "But yourself could be telling me if its passing this way again you'll be today."

"I shall," she said, and glanced at her wrist where a scrap of golden chain held a watch small enough to be put in a man's ear and him never to be knowing of it. "In about an hour."

And then the Devil, his work done, released her feet and let her be about her business and Sean, with an hour to wait, wandered through tiny streets and crooked lanes and wondered how it was that the sun shone brighter and that the very air seemed to glitter with suspended gems.

And so it was that he met the Dealer in Dreams.

* * * *

A smiling man is the Dealer in Dreams and he has reason to smile. He smiled even wider as Sean pushed open the door of his shop and stood blinking in the soft light, so that it seemed the two men were trying each to outdo the other with their good humour. He smiled and rubbed his hands and leaned on his counter and his voice was as soft as eider and as sweet as the scent of roses.

"May I help you, sir?"

Sean had met men before who smiled and spoke like that and never had good for him come from the meeting but his head was filled with beauty and the soul of him was tickled at what he had read. And not even the good God Himself could have stopped a man like Sean O'Donnell from being curious about the lettering he had read on the window of the tiny shop.

"A fine day to you," greeted Sean and nodded towards the window. "And is it a fine joke you would be playing at all?"

"No joke," said the Dealer and if his eyes twinkled a little the brighter and his smile grew a little the wider then surely he could not be blamed for that?

"It's a long way that I've travelled," said Sean. "And many a strange thing I have seen since I left Ballinasloe.

But never the Devil of a thing have I seen the like of this."
And he smiled with the wonder of it.

"There are many strange things to be seen by a man
who has the eye to see them," said the Dealer. "There are
many odd corners in the world, and other worlds, which
hide stranger businesses than mine. Or perhaps you doubt
my word?"

"I do not," said Sean and meant every word of it. The
Dealer was a strange one to be sure but what of that? There
were many strange folk walking the ways of the world and
if a man wanted to buy, sell and exchange dreams then that
was his business even if it was one with Devil the bit of
sense in it. But, still and all, it was a strange thing and good
for a tale on a winters night when the wind was screaming
like a banshee and the peat hissed in the grate and the talk
had run dry. And he had an hour to spare and where was the
harm in talking to the queer creature with the queer trade?

"Then it's meaning it that you are?" asked Sean just to
be sure.

"I mean it," said the Dealer and smiled as if he had met
men who doubted their eyes before, as indeed he had. "I
will buy a dream if you have one to sell. I will sell a dream
if you are willing to buy. And I will exchange a dream if that
should be your wish." He coughed as if reluctant to touch
on the matter. "With any necessary adjustments, naturally."

"Naturally," agreed Sean, though why the smiling man
should be talking of dreams as if he were talking of pigs and
hens was something he couldn't get to the bottom of. He
was about to say so when a bell chimed from somewhere
behind the curtains which divided the rear of the shop and
the Dealer stepped towards them.

"A business call," he apologised, "If you will be so kind
as to wait?"

"I will do that," said Sean, and stood where he was as the Dealer vanished then, alone, he stared about him with eyes as big and as wondering as those of a child taken into the biggest toy shop in the world and surely he couldn't be blamed for that?

Jars stood on shelves against the walls. Hundreds of jars on dozens of shelves. Big jars and small jars, some of clouded glass, and some of ancient stone, some with long thin necks and others as squat and as fat as tubs of butter. Metal jars there were shining as if made of beaten brass or of polished gold. Amber jars and jars of glinting ice. Jars of every shape and size and colour that a man could imagine and some that no man could imagine at all. And, with only Sean himself in the shop which was almost too small to hold another, split as it was by the counter, and with himself not moving and hardly breathing at all, and with the shop away from all traffic and outside noises, it should have been as quiet as a grave. But quiet it was not.

From all sides came the most peculiar collection of sounds ever heard by mortal man. Sighs as if from broken hearts, laughter as if from happy children, deep groans and tittering giggles, baby chuckles and muffled screams, gurgling and whimpering, moaning and keening, singing and whispering, all merging and mixing as if he were listening to the life-noises of a world. And all the sounds seemed to come from the jars.

It was an odd thing and a strange thing and Sean crossed himself and muttered a charm the Old Woman of Ballinasloe had taught him and which was to be used when he heard the scampering of the little people for fear that they should do him a harm. That done, and as safe as a man could ever be in the world, curiosity pricked him so that he reached out a long arm and rested his hand on one of the jars and was lifting it from its place when he heard the sound of a cough just behind him. Quick as a flash he let loose the jar and spun on his heel and smiled at the Dealer for it was not a good thing to be prying into another man's belongings and him queer in the head.

"You were going to open that jar," said the Dealer.

"I was not," said Sean.

"You were going to steal it then."

"I was not," protested Sean. "It was after looking at it that I was and that was all." He glanced towards the door wondering if he could reach it and escape without doing the Dealer harm for the smiling man no longer smiled and his eyes held more than just a twinkle. Then the tubby man smiled again and his eyes sparkled and he was all friendliness and good humour and things were almost as they were before. But not quite though it would have taken a sharp ear to have noticed the difference. For now the air was no longer filled with the sounds of the world, only the soft footsteps of the Dealer as he moved behind his counter.

"You will pardon me," he said. "There is a most urgent matter, a question of a dream for a—a client."

Sean watched as the Dealer busied himself at his work. From beneath the counter he took a phial of polished jet and then ran his eye over his jars.

"Let me see now," mused the Dealer. "Some baby's laughter I think and, yes, a touch of lovers sighs." He reached and selected and placed two of the jars against his phial and, as he did so, the sounds of chuckles and sighs filled the air to die as he replaced the jars in their places.

"Always a good background," he said cheerfully to Sean. "And cheap too." He pursed his lips again like a cook selecting a rare dish to set before a king. "Now what? A touch of horror should go well." He sighed as he selected a tiny black jar. "The sobs of condemned men, rare and terribly difficult to obtain but there, we can't do without it." And Sean felt sweat bead his forehead as he heard what came out of the jar.

"Some tears and some groans, some love and some hate, a dash of hope and a soupcon of despair, a touch of bitterness and a helping of futility. Shake, add a generous measure of you know what," and here the Dealer winked like all the Satyrs which ever were, "and the dream is ready." He stared fondly at the tiny phial in his hand.

* * * *

It is a grievous thing to be a disappointed man and Sean was that very thing. Sure and the Old Woman of Ballinasloe could have done as well with her brews and not made half the fuss about it and not called what she sold by so grand a name as this smiling man did. And almost Sean walked out of the shop but there were the jars and the queer sounds he had heard and— Sure and all, the Devil found a useful tool when he found curiosity in a man's heart.

"And would there be no more to it than that?" asked Sean. "Just a tiny bottle with something in it? Faith, and I'd sell you a dream made of poteen which would take you to the ends of the world and back again and you feeling every step of the way."

"This?" The Dealer tossed the phial from hand to hand and shrugged. "This is just a minor sample of my art. The mainstay of my trade, as it were. Dreams for a night or a week or even a year. Dreams for those with soft lives and hard thoughts who are jaded of their own sensations. Temporary dreams for those who know not how to dream without my aid. Brief respite for those without imagination and for others it is best not to name. But do not judge me on this."

"On what then? For sure it's a big claim you are making for a thing so small."

"Small?" The dealer did not lose his smile but his eyes lost a scrap of their twinkle. "Is it a small thing to make a beggar dream that he is a king? Or a king dream that he is a beggar? Is it a little thing to give love to the loveless, horror to the unterrified, hope to those who are strangers to mercy? Would you call that small?"

"I would not," said Sean.

"But that is nothing." Casually the Dealer tossed the phial into a drawer, closing it softly and smiling as he raised his head. "I deal in dreams, not mere sensations. I can give an old man a dream which will make him young again and I can give a young man a dream which will fill his pockets with gold." And here the Dealer's eyes glowed like fiery stars. "Would you be needing such a dream?"

"I would not," said Sean.

"No?" The Dealer laughed, a man-of-the-world laugh and his eyes were bold as they stared at the O'Donnell. "You are young and handsome but that is not enough. Youth dies and looks fade and then what is left? Dreams are poor things with which to win the heart of an attractive girl and few dreams can fill a man's stomach or put clothes on his back. You are young, my friend, and you have a dream, but of what use is that dream to you?" And he left the question in the air while the Devil whispered in Sean's ear.

* * * *

For sure and what the Dealer said was true enough. Fine dreams had Sean but Devil the gold in his pocket and he'd starved more times than he had eaten his fill. Not that it had worried him even if he'd thought about it which was less than often. The world was as it was and the sun shone on a rich man as it did on a poor and it was a grand thing to be walking with the whole day to be spent in the walking and **to** be seeing with a poet's eye and to be talking to the trees and the rustling grass and to be taking things as they came with never a care at all.

And for sure the smiling man was queer in the head for him to be talking of the buying of something of no value at all and for him to be talking of gold for the buying of it. And more than talking by the look of him, standing there with a great ring in his hand and his eyes twinkling and himself bubbling with good humour. And it would be a rare thing to sell him nothing for that gold and to be walking away laughing after it with money to spend and a grand tale to be telling when the bitter wind keened and the peat hissed and the talk ran dry.

"Take this ring," said the Dealer. "Sell me your dream for this ring."

"I will not," said Sean, and laughed at the look of him. "My dream is a good dream and worth more than your gold."

"You think that I am joking," said the Dealer. He added a second ring to the first. "I am not joking. Take these rings and sell me your dream."

"I will that," said Sean, and laughed again as he thought of pigs and hens. "But my dream is a good dream and what would I be doing without a dream at all?"

"I'll exchange your dream," urged the Dealer. "I'll give you a dream and these two rings for the dream which you will sell to me."

"And would it be a good dream?" said Sean, and he felt his sides ache as he thought about it. "It's not any old dream that I'll be taking for what you want to buy."

"It is a well-tried and well-used dream," said the Dealer. "It is a dream which most men have or most men grow into. The chances are that you will grow into it yourself before long. Will you accept it?"

"I will that," said Sean.

"Then it is done," said the Dealer. And without more ado he thrust the rings into Sean's hand and pushed him towards the door and out of the shop and into the street.

And the odd part about it was that when Sean looked back at where he had been he couldn't see the tiny shop at all.

* * * *

Not that he worried about it for time was passing and he had to be where a wonderful colleen would be passing with her bold eye and figure which caught the breath in his throat and the saucy way of walking which would have earned her hard words and sharp looks had she been back in Ballinasloe.

But despite his hurry the rings had to be examined and it was with relief that he felt the metal give beneath his teeth and knew that they were of gold and not of brass. And he frowned as he bit them, wondering how it was that he had not tested them before for the fine fool he would have been had they turned out to be a pig in a poke. Then he hesitated to decide what they would be fetching and his eye fell on a motor car and he felt a sudden stab of wanting for the shiny thing; himself who had never wanted other than his own legs before.

A window gave on a fine show of soft furniture and he hesitated again, wanting a soft bed and a fine rug for the floor and one of those things which gave a man music and pictures in his room. Then he saw what was wanted for the fine things and worried lest the rings should not fetch enough then cheered at the thought that he could lend the money and make more money by the lending of it. And it seemed a fine thing to him to be making the money and then more money so that he could be having all the things offered in the shops and then a house to put them in and servants to wait on him so that he could live like a rich man.

The thought gripped him so that he no longer saw the beauty of the sun or smelt the scent of the air nor did he see the bright colours around him or the smiling faces of the flowers growing, few to be sure, but growing bravely despite that in the few pots and boxes on the windows. And he frowned as he thought so that he was at the place before he knew it and there was the colleen and her coming towards him with a smile and a warmth in her eye and a blush on her cheek and him not answering her smile at all.

"I waited," she said, and then lost her smile as she looked at him. And now she saw what she had not seen before, what the brave dream inside of him had made of no importance at his frayed jacket and the two inches of wrist, at the broken shoes and the poorness of him, and seeing this she turned away.

For now he had only a common dream and was only a common man.

DEAR GHOST

I stepped carefully into the transport and felt the sickening wrench as it sent me half-way around the world. With the wrench came the old, familiar fear. *This time*? *This time*? The fear was illogical, never yet had anyone failed to reach their destination but I couldn't remember to forget what would happen if anything went wrong.

Curtis was waiting when I arrived. I saw him as the door of the cubicle slid aside, sitting at his big desk, his grey hair a tumbled mess, his grey face lined with strain and fatigue. He looked up as I came towards him.

"Nugent! You made good time."

"Speed of light." I stood staring down at him waiting for him to get to the point. I didn't have to wait long.

"Nugent, I want you to take out a starship."

I didn't say anything. I didn't have to.

"I know that you've done your time, but this is an emergency."

I headed back towards the transport.

"John! Please!"

That stopped me. Not what he said so much as the way he said it. Curtis never appealed to anyone. Never. He told them and they did it. Or he told them and they didn't do it in which case they never had a second opportunity to refuse. I came back towards the desk.

"What's the matter, Curtis, you want to send me ghost?"

"You've still time in hand. You could make the trip easily."

"And back?"

"Molendis is a nice planet, John."

"Earth is better."

"Earth is the best," he agreed, and sat looking down at his hands. "You know that I wouldn't have sent for you if it hadn't been necessary."

"Definition of words. What is 'necessary' to you needn't be to me." I should have walked out then but something, curiosity maybe, forced me to stay. "What is this emergency?"

"There's been an outbreak of *colthin* on Molendis. It's a new planet and hasn't the laboratories and techniques to process and prepare the vaccine. We did that for them here on Earth and now we've got to get it to them."

"Simple, send it in the normal way." I stared at him. "Don't tell me that you've got no ships."

"We have ships, John. We need a pilot."

"But why me?"

This time it was his turn to remain silent and I thought I knew why. Pilots were scarce, scarcer than ships because ships lasted longer than men. It took a long time to train a man so that he could find his way through the swirling distortion of hyper-space. And it took men to do it, machines were affected too much by the drive-field.

"This is ridiculous," I said. "There must be more than one pilot on Earth at this time. You don't really need me."

"I think we do, John," he said quietly. And then I got it.

"Expendable! You think that I'm expendable! Damn you, Curtis!"

"Damn me if you like," he said, still calm. "But what about Molendis? You want me to send a new pilot there with the chance that he will bring *colthin* back with him? Have you ever seen what that disease can do? On Molendis it must be bad but on Earth…" He shook his head. "I can't take the risk. I dare not. Molendis is in quarantine for the next ten years and the vaccine will be the last cargo they'll receive for that period. It's up to you whether they get it or not."

He meant it and I hated him for leaving the decision to me. Now I knew why he looked so drawn why, despite all logic to the contrary, he was willing to make one last contact with the disease-ridden planet. I'd never seen the full effects of *colthin,* no one had, but up to date it had depopulated three worlds and decimated ten. They were frontier planets with plenty of open space and individual isolation. What it would do to Earth with its crowded cities and teeming population no one liked to think.

"Molendis is how far? Thirty?"

"Forty-two and a half."

"And I've a maximum of fifty hours." I looked out of the windows to where the sun was painting the soaring spires of the city with red and gold, pink and delicate orange. Across the blue sky a few clouds drifted like engineless ships and, in the distance, I could see a touch of green. Suddenly I didn't want to leave Earth again, ever.

"You're asking too much, Curtis. No matter which way you look at it I don't stand a chance. How far is the nearest planet from Molendis?"

"Fifteen."

"So I stay there or go ghost, is that it?"

"Yes, John. That's about it."

He didn't say any more. He didn't try to beg or plead or mention that ten million people were depending on me to give them a fighting chance. He didn't even mention that I owed a duty to the race. He didn't have to.

I was going to take out the ship.

* * * *

It was old and, like me, expendable. It stood a little to one side of the field as if ashamed and, as I stood at the open hatchway after my pre-flight check up, I stared towards the new ships, the big ones, tall and sleek and as haughty as a woman. But no matter how good they looked now they were all sisters beneath the skin. They, like the crews who ran them, were sll operating on vanishing time. Curtis was waiting for me at the foot of the ladder.

"Everything all right, John?"

"Seems to be."

He nodded, his grey face masked and expressionless, and I wondered just how it must feel to sit behind a desk and play at God. I didn't envy Curtis, sometimes sitting behind a desk can be the hardest thing there is, especially when you've a galaxy, an expanding race, and constantly diminishing ships and men to co-ordinate and intermesh the destinies of half a hundred worlds.

A group of youngsters passed close to us. Fresh cadets from the Academy, still wet behind the ears and all suffering from the impatience of youth. I stared after them, remembering the time when I'd been as they were. It seemed a long, long time ago.

"You've seen the vaccine release?" Curtis spoke as if the words burned his mouth. "You can unload as soon as you touch down without unsealing the ship."

"I've seen it." I stared at him. "What's the point? Does it matter if I unseal or not?" Something about the way he avoided my eyes made me step close to him. "Curtis! Just how bad is it on Molendis?"

"Bad," he admitted. "We were late getting the news and it's taken time to prepare the vaccine. *Colthin* is fast, John, fast and nasty." He looked away. "But we must do what we can."

"We?" I didn't mean to say it and when I saw his expression I wished that I hadn't. Regrets were useless. Even if every living soul on the planet were already dead we still had to try. Because we couldn't be sure. No one could, and if the vaccine could save a half of one percent, even if it could save a tenth of that, we still had to try. That's the way we're made.

"You can unload the cases in the central plaza and, if things look too bad, you can take off and head for one of the uninhabited regions." He was talking nonsense, and he knew it. "It's all I can offer, John," he said miserably. "I'm sorry."

"Is that why the ship's loaded with supplies?" I had wondered about that. "Near-ghost stuff I suppose?"

"Yes, John."

"The ship too." I looked back and upwards to where it waited. "You must have raided the graveyard for all that."

He shrugged, not answering, but I didn't need an answer. Expendable pilot, expendable ship, expendable supplies. Curtis was making certain that Molendis would stay in quarantine.

A siren cut through the silence between us and a red light began flashing a series of longs and shorts from the control tower. I didn't have to study them to know they were spelling out my signal. Time to go. Time to head out for the last time. Time to leave Earth—forever.

"Goodbye, John." Curtis's hand was warm and hard against my own. "Goodbye, and thank you."

I watched him walk away. I didn't repeat his thanks—how can you thank your own executioner? But I felt a vague regret that I would never see him again. I liked Curtis. I would always like him.

Sighing I turned towards the waiting ship.

Take off was as usual. The ship was old but, like all her breed, she had been built well. I lifted her gently, using more fuel than I might, but remembering the cases of vaccine. Take-off shock could do more than damage the packing, it could cause degeneration in the actual vaccine itself and anyway, I wasn't in that much of a hurry.

I levelled off at a hundred thousand miles and began to hunt for the target stars. The Moon was the other side of Earth so it didn't bother me and, as I'd risen in the shadow, the sun wasn't too much of a nuisance. Finding my bearings didn't take long and I blasted towards my destination, building up some forward velocity before engaging the field and dropping into hyper-drive.

On the panel before me the meters kicked and a green lamp flashed to give the all clear. I dropped my hand on the button then, just before pressing it, I took a long, last look at familiar places.

Then I pressed the button and, as the rainbow pattern of hyper-space swirled against the visi-screen, I started on the last fifty hours of my life.

Fifty hours in hyper-space that is, but all pilots and starship crews measure their lives that way. Five thousand hours plus or minus five. Five thousand light years of travel, plus or minus five. The sum total of ship expectancy for any man or woman in the starfleet.

And I'd less than fifty left to go.

Vanishing time we called it, and it was the price we had to pay for breaking the Einsteinian equations. In order to travel faster than light we had to take the ship somewhere out of the normal universe. The field did that, never mind how, and in that strange region of swirling light we travelled a light year an hour. It was wonderful, but it had a catch.

You can't play about with mass and you can't get something for nothing. There was a constant strain, a weakening, vibration, energy loss, call it what you like but it all added up to the same thing. After five thousand hours of hyperdrive travel a man went ghost. After twenty thousand hours a ship went the same way. Organic matter five thousand, inorganic twenty. Simple.

Except for those who lived on vanishing time.

Because no one knew exactly what happened when a man went ghost. He didn't die, not as we know death, but he didn't live either, not as we know life. He simply vanished. Food, water, clothing, all went the same way after five thousand hours. Metal, ships, fuel, wire followed fifteen thousand hours later. They winked oat. They disappeared. As far as normality was concerned they ceased to exist.

There were theories, of course, there always are. The scientists said that normal matter, vibrated by the field, somehow reached the breaking point and became transmuted into some form of negative matter. An atom is a small thing surrounded by space and, if that atom should somehow suffer energy loss or actual displacement, then matter as we know it ceases to exist. In effect it moves somewhere else, where is anyone's guess. They could have been right, I wouldn't know, but pilots, crews, all those who worked on, handled or knew about starships had a simpler term. They called it going 'ghost'.

* * * *

I tried not to think about it. Five thousand hours isn't a long time, certainly not long enough to compensate for ten years of solid training. New pilots were constantly being trained, and as constantly being transferred to the interplanet ships when they had served their starship time. New ships were constantly being built, only to be relegated in the same way. The system was fine for interplanetary communications, but trying to maintain contact with the expanding frontiers as well as intermesh the settled star systems was like trying to scoop up water with a sieve.

I sat for a while staring at the visi-screen and letting myself calm down. Feeling the way I did it would only take a touch to make me collapse the field, reverse the ship and head back to Earth while I could still make it. Or I could head towards one of the nearer stars, there were plenty within twenty light years, and sneak back later. The only trouble with that was that I'd have to live with myself later, and somehow I knew that I wouldn't like that sort of a man to live with.

So I checked the ship instead.

It was big, too big for one man, and had only recently been resurrected from the graveyard. That's what we called the place where ships and supplies were sent after service. Using the metal again was too dangerous for contemplation. It might get incorporated into a starship and blink out when least expected. It wouldn't be funny to have half the hull disappear while in hyper-space. So, after they had hauled their last cargo between the planets, the old ships were swung into orbit and sent on automatic into hyper-space. Like me the ship was expendable.

The food lockers were surprisingly well filled. I wondered about that. Did Curtis have his own ideas of what happened when a man went ghost? And was he providing for me in case I should? From the stores I wandered over the ship in general. As yet there was nothing for me to do, the hard part would come later when I had to sort the one specific pattern of Molendis from all the others. It wasn't easy, the differences were minute, and a mistake could emerge the ship parsecs from its destination. Remember that minutes saved on each trip could extend the vanishing time of the vessel and you know why pilots had to be well trained.

The shock came when I entered a cabin. I had expected it to be empty, it was, but not in the way I had imagined. It was devoid of human life but not of human presence. There were some garments in a locker, some things still on the bulkhead table, held by their magnetic bases. There was a photograph on the wall and a faint but unmistakable aura of perfume. The photograph gave me the answer.

It was that of a woman. Smiling, pert, brown-haired and brown-eyed. She must have been about twenty, ten years younger than myself, and she was beautiful.

I looked at it. It was the natural response of a man who had only just recently given up the idea of marriage and a normal life. I'd had big plans for my future, plans which had all gone into the discard, but I was still human and still susceptible. There was something about the photograph, something familiar, and I frowned as I stared at it.

I was still frowning when the lights dimmed, something cold touched one ear and something else brushed against one cheek.

I didn't jump, or run, or scream. Instead I stood quite still and listened to the pounding of my heart. Fear *is* a peculiar emotion, even when we know that there is nothing to be afraid of, still the body responds. We carry too large a heritage of the past to wholly throw off the primitive reactions. The ship was empty, I knew that, and I knew that there could only be one logical explanation of what had happened.

The ship was haunted.

* * * *

Ghosts were nothing new. I stood a good chance of becoming one myself, but up to now I'd only heard of haunted ships, I'd never actually travelled in one. There were tales in plenty, of invisible crews, invisible pilots, crewmen who had gone ghost and who still remained with their ships. Most of them were obvious fabrications but it was cold fact that people had gone ghost and, if they had, was it possible that they still remained with the ships to haunt them?

I decided to experiment.

"Who are you?" I didn't expect an answer and I wasn't disappointed. "Is that you?" I pointed towards the photograph. The lights brightened and I took it to mean 'yes.' I looked around, there was nothing to see, of course, but I was strangely reluctant to leave the cabin.

"Can you hear me?" No reaction. "Can you see me?" The same result. I asked a few more questions feeling more and more foolish as I stood before the photograph and talked to empty air. The lights didn't dim again, nothing chilled or touched me, and I felt that I was wasting my time.

Sheer curiosity made me go through the things in the cabin. There were some intimate feminine underwear, a couple of dresses, some cosmetics, perfumes, a little jewellery, and a complete nurse's uniform. I touched it, it felt somehow old as if it had been hanging there for a long time and, even as I watched, it disappeared from under my hand.

Startled, I stepped back and, even as I did so, the other garments began to go ghost. The photograph went last of all, the frame hanging empty against the wall. Foolishly I stared at it, than at the items of jewellery, the inorganic caps of the cosmetic bottles, the scraps of metal and wire left behind.

I decided to get back to work.

It wasn't easy. I kept seeing a pert, brown-eyed face pictured against the screens and, every time I saw it, I had a sense of familiarity. Somewhere I had seen that face before but for the life of me I couldn't tell where. It worried me a little, that sense of familiarity, and I tried to think of something else.

The ship, for instance. I knew that it had been resurrected from the graveyard but the feminine garments and other stuff in the cabin didn't make sense. It had gone ghost too soon for it to have always travelled with the ship and, thinking of it, I began to get a crazy idea. Suppose someone had deliberately stocked the ship with the possessions of someone who had gone ghost in her? The entire vessel was near the end of its vanishing time, supplies too, and that couldn't have happened by accident. Someone had arranged for everything to be the way it was and, as far as I was concerned, there was only one man who could do that. Curtis!

Thinking of him I knew that I was right and, thinking of him, I knew where I had seen that photograph before. It was the twin to one he kept on his desk. The girl? I'd heard something somewhere. His wife? His sister? I snapped my fingers. Curtis's sister had gone ghost in the early days before they knew what it was all about. The ship was haunted by Shellia Curtis.

I felt sad as I thought about it. Curtis was pushing seventy and his sister must have been born about the same decade as he was. No wonder the garments had felt old. They had probably been in store for something like fifty years.

So much for my dreams of romance.

I concentrated on my job and tried to forget the vanishing hours of my life. I ate, and it didn't surprise me to find that a good half of the stores had winked out of existence. I slept a little, though sleep wasn't easy, and I forced myself to roam the creaking corridors of the ship. She was well built but she was old and, during the course of her life, had developed odd creaks and slithers unnoticeable during normal flight, but startlingly loud to a man on his own. I'm not particularly nervous, but I'm no hero either, and I was getting to the stage where I was walking about with my head on my shoulders half the time, when the alarm rang.

That would mean Molendis.

* * * *

Emerging took the usual time and the usual cold-sweat of anticipation. Either we made it or we didn't. Either the ship emerged in empty space or there would be a big blue flash as two objects tried to occupy the same space at the same time. My luck held, my astrogation had been good, and I fired the main drive towards the big, green and brown planet a million miles towards the glowing, blue-white sun.

I heard the radio warning as soon as I cut in the receiver. It was short, sharp, and unmistakable. It spelt quarantine, death, and isolation. It spelt *colthin,* and, any other ship hearing it, would immediately streak away to other places. I just kept on going.

I'd hit atmosphere before the strident signals faded to be replaced by the weary tones of a man either too ill, or too indifferent to feel emotion.

"Warning. This planet is rotten with *colthin.* Do not land. Do not land."

"I'm coming in," I said cheerfully. "Stand by to receive vaccine."

"Vaccine!" He sounded as though I'd shown him the Holy Grail. "You've got it?"

"That's right."

"That's wrong!" His enthusiasm ran away like water in a punctured barrel. "It's too late."

"It can't be too late." I swung into orbit and began to lose velocity. "You're alive, aren't you?"

"Am I?" He didn't laugh but if he had it wouldn't have been through amusement. "Maybe I am. So are a few other people. Damn few. A couple of weeks ago the vaccine might have done some good but now…"

"Is it that bad?" I braked hard and kicked in the stabilisers. Below me the city spread in neat regularity and I headed towards the main plaza. I didn't think anyone would object to my blast searing their flower beds.

"You'll see," he said grimly, then coughed. I didn't like the way he did that.

I didn't like what I saw after I settled either.

Men aren't really dignified but when they're walking and talking and remembering that they're human, you can pretend they are. But you can't pretend when they come crawling towards you in every stage of loathsome disease. I stared at them through the high-mag screen and I knew then why no normal ship could have been sent to Molendis.

They were rotting as they moved.

Colthin seemed to combine the worst symptoms of everything that was bad. I stared at them and felt myself wanting to be sick. I stared at them and tried to remember what Earth had looked like when I left and not what it would be like if someone ever imported *colthin* with his cargo. I felt sorry, sure, I wanted to help. Hell that was why I was here, but I just couldn't help myself.

I triggered the release and dropped part of my cargo then, with the same movement of my hand, I blasted up and away from what was below.

There were three other big cities, distribution points for the vaccine—if anyone was alive and able to distribute it. I orbited the planet too, spilling out antibiotics in a fine, pervading stream so that the airborne virus of the disease could be rendered harmless. Then, my job done, I settled down on a gentle slope close to what had once been a thriving village and took time off to think.

I was safe from *colthin* while I remained inside the ship. Once I stepped out on the planet, even with the vaccine, I only had a fifty-fifty chance. Normally I would have taken that chance but one thing stopped me. Where was I going to live?

The cities, from what I had seen of them, were hopeless. The air, aside from the warning signal, was dead. I'd seen no ground transport, no air-transport, no one working the fields. I'd seen maybe ten thousand people in the final stages of the disease and, of them, I wanted no part.

There were others, of course, there had to be. Even with *colthin* as virulent as it was, yet there should have been some people immune. They had probably run to the uninhabited regions and were waiting for the epidemic to burn itself out and, with those, I might be able to get along. The trick was to find them.

Molendis, like all newly developed planets, had a high concentration at several key points. That was inevitable when you realise that all the initial machine tools had to be imported. The colonists would only spread slowly out to the other regions, breaking ground, developing farms, starting mines and factories as they went. Ten million people isn't a really big population for an Earth-sized planet, not when most of them lived in the cities with the servo-mechs and automatic factories providing most of the staples.

Another century would have seen the planet evenly populated, a half-century even if emigration had increased, but they hadn't had that time to play with. *Colthin* had caught them just at the wrong moment of their planetary culture and their very concentration had written their finish. And I was sitting right in the middle of it.

* * * *

It took two weeks for them to find me. Two weeks in which I waited and kidded myself that the waiting served a purpose. I knew that the antibiotics I'd dropped would be busy clearing the air but I also knew it was only a prophylactic measure. The only way to beat *coltbin* was to let it die out for want of hosts and, no matter how long I waited, I was still a potential host. In five years I would be safe, the quarantine period was double that for safety, but I couldn't wait five years. Not and remain sane.

The first three days it wasn't so bad—bad that is in relation to what came after. I had food, water, and an entire ship to move about in and nothing to do. That was the worst part, I had nothing to do. I tried the complete band of the radio and could only get the warning signal. I caught up on my sleep, did a few exercises, and tried to forget the ship was haunted. But the ghost wouldn't let me.

It wasn't anything she did, the episode of the dimming lights was never repeated, but I just couldn't forget a pert, brown-eyed face and the knowledge that she had gone ghost in this very ship. Telling myself that she had been born sixty years ago didn't do any good. I hadn't seen her as an old woman, no one had, and to me she was just like her photograph.

Inevitably I began talking to her.

There's a lot of nonsense talked and written about spacemen. It's a popular assumption that we are strong, silent characters who are never so happy as when we're on our own. That's pure bunk. There is enough loneliness in space without wanting more. The stars are too far away, the journeys too long, the hyper-drive too worrying for any man not to want company of his own kind. And I was alone in a creaking old ship on a planet which, as far as I knew, was devoid of life. What else could I do?

It helped, somehow, to hear the sound of my own voice. I talked to her when I was preparing a meal. I talked to her when I checked the instruments. It got so that I was talking to her all the time. I didn't answer myself, I wasn't that bad, but I knew that it was only a matter of time.

"I'll give them another week, Shellia," I said on the tenth day. Already I thought of her as Shellia. "If they don't come then we'll move the ship somewhere else. Yes?"

No reply, of course, how could there be? But somehow that didn't matter.

It didn't matter anyway because at the end of the second week they arrived.

There were five of them, three men and two women. I heard them call over the external microphones and almost broke my neck getting up to control and switching on the high-mag screen. They were rough, the men whiskered, all dirty and in rags, but they were whole and without any signs of *colthin*. I could have kissed them. Especially I could have kissed the women.

"Hey there!" One of them, a man, apparently the leader, stared up at the ship and yelled towards me. "Anyone at home?"

"Yes." I sent my amplified voice towards them. "Where are you from?"

"Nowhere. We ran out before the plague could get us. Man! Are we glad to see you."

"Me too. Any more of you?"

"No, just us." He turned and said something to the others. "Open up will you."

"Sure." I stabbed at the hatch-button and waited for the double doors to swing open. They didn't. I tried again with the same result.

"Shellia!" I was annoyed and my voice must have showed it. "Quit messing around. I want to go out."

Funny how I automatically thought to blame Shellia. There was no apparent reason for the hatch not opening, but a dozen things could have caused it from a sticking relay to a total power-loss. I stabbed at the button again and fumed, then, still fuming, I got down to tracing the fault. While I was doing it I had time to think.

I thought of Curtis, and the Chinese and their habit of sending cash and material to their dead. I thought of a ship which was due at any time to go ghost, and of myself who was in the same position. And, as I thought, I began to get the glimmering of a startling idea. Molendis was a ruined world, and Curtis must have known that I'd be too late. He must have known too that life on a disease-ridden world wouldn't appeal to me. Had he intended for both me and the ship to go ghost?

Had he intended to provide for his sister?

The concept was ludicrous and yet, was it? There had been a lot of investigation by the scientists on just what happened when men and materials went ghost. Had they found out something unknown to the majority? Curtis would know, he was in a position to know everything, and rumour had it that he had deeply loved his sister and had never really recovered from her loss. Maybe he'd had the bright idea of sending me after her to keep her company.

But I wasn't going to play.

Not when there were real, living people outside and the chance of a real, living existence. Whatever happened when a man went ghost couldn't compensate for the total loss of life as we know it. I was still young, still able to enjoy things and I had no intention of blinking out for a long, long time yet.

I found the fault, a stuck relay, and I fixed it in half a second. Why it had stuck was a mystery, there was no apparent reason for the breakdown, and I wasted no more time getting back to control. I pressed the button, the doors whined open, and, for the first time, I breathed the warm, scented air of Molendis.

I'd already loaded myself with vaccine so I wasn't really worried. It was worth taking the fifty-fifty chance in order to hear a real, human voice again. Impatiently I waited for them to climb aboard.

Carter, who was the leader, came first. He was followed by Gerald and Henson and after him came the two women. They crowded the control cabin and I led the way down to the rec-room and broke out some food. Over the meal we passed introductions and general chitchat. The real business came over coffee.

"What are your plans, Nugent?" Carter wiped his bearded mouth with the back of his hand and stretched his legs in animal satisfaction.

"That's up to you. Do you want me to join up with you, or do you want me to move on?"

"Move on where?" Hanson picked at his teeth and watched me from narrowed eyes.

"South, north, half-way round the planet." I gestured towards the hull. "I don't know. Anywhere I can find people will do."

"There aren't any people." Gerald made as if he was going to spit on the floor. "Hell, man! You circled the world, did you see any?"

"No," I admitted. "But there must be some somewhere."

"Not on Molendis." Carter shrugged. "They all flocked to the cities when *colthin* struck. They wanted help, vaccine, anything to beat the plague. As far as I know we are the only living persons on the planet."

I believed him. I had to believe him. I hadn't seen any proof to the contrary and it was logical to assume that anyone who'd seen or heard the ship would have come running. I remembered the radio operator and what I had seen in the cities.

"How did you escape?"

"We were out on an expedition. I'd located a vein of uranium and wanted to plot it before filing claim. We had a medical kit and a little vaccine. When we heard the news we decided to stay isolated." Carter shrugged. "There were twenty in the original party."

"And the rest?"

He didn't answer and he didn't have to. I could guess what had happened. The vaccine had been reserved for the elite. When the others had been stricken they had been left to rot and die. Nice man, Carter.

"So we're back to the beginning," I said. "Four men, two women, and isolation for the next ten years. Nice prospect."

"It could be better," said Carter softly. "You've a ship and a universe to rove in. Why don't we just up and move?"

"You mean leave here and land on some uninhabited world?"

"Sure, why not?"

"And take *colthin* with us?"

"We haven't got *colthin*," snapped Gerald. "If we had we'd be dead by now. We're clean, all of us, why the hell should we stay here?"

"You can't be sure of that," I pointed out. "You could be a carrier, anything. Damn it man! You've seen what happened here. Do you want to spread it somewhere else?"

They didn't answer that but from the way they looked at each other I could see that I was wasting my breath. Carter shifted a little in his chair and one of the women sniggered.

"Look," he said gently. "Let's not have any trouble about this. If you want to stay here no one's going to stop you. We're getting out, and no one's going to stop us. Do you help us or..." The pistol he slowly produced from a pocket finished the sentence for him.

"This is a one-planet sun," I said. "Where do you hope to reach?"

"Anywhere with air and water, cities and people." He gestured with the pistol. "Hell, man! I'm not particular. Just set us down on a liveable world, one with some people on it, and we'll be satisfied."

"And *colthin*?"

"We haven't got it. We won't be taking it with us."

He lied and he knew it but he just didn't care. For the first time I had cause to thank Curtis. He had foreseen this and, though they didn't know it, they would never use the ship to get anywhere. It would go ghost and leave them breathing space. The trouble was that I'd go ghost too.

But the pistol in Carter's hand left me no alternative.

* * * *

I warmed the main drive and strapped myself in. I sealed the ship and made the preliminary warning. I took a last look at green grass and blue sky and then, before I could weaken, I hit the buttons and lifted us towards the waiting stars. I wasn't gentle and there was no reason for me to save fuel. I slammed us up at a nine-G acceleration and took a perverse pleasure at the thought of the damage I was causing my unwanted passengers. Carter swore at me after I'd cut the drive.

"What the hell are you trying to do, kill us?"

"No." I leaned back in the chair. "Where to now?"

"How far's the nearest planet?"

"Fifteen light years, but they won't let us land. This entire area for thirty lights will be alerted and watching for unauthorised landings."

"That applies anywhere," he said and I reminded myself not to be too smart. "Take us to a place towards the Rim. The new worlds aren't so particular."

"Phoriphor? That's about fifty lights out."

"It'll do." He sat down and nursed the pistol. "I'm watching you, Nugent. Be smart and I'll rip your stomach open. Be sensible and you can string along with us." He grinned. "Don't forget that you're in the same boat as we are now."

He was wrong, but he didn't know that. He knew and I knew that anyone breaking quarantine would be shot on sight but that was the least of my worries. I spun the gyros as I aligned the ship on the star sights, I selected a couple at random, and then hesitated with my hand on the field drive button.

"You're sure that you want to do this, Carter?"

"Sure I'm sure." He gestured with the pistol. "Get moving." I sighed and pressed the button.

Hyper-space swirled around us, a glittering rainbow pattern on the screens and, as I stared at it, I felt my life slipping away. Fifty hours maximum. Minus forty-three left seven and most likely two. In two to seven hours I would go ghost.

"What's the matter with you?" Carter was staring at me. "You sick or something?"

I touched my face, it was wet with perspiration, and my reflected image in the polished control panel showed me a sight I didn't like. It isn't easy for a man to count the hours of his life, it was a thing I'd lived with ever since my first starflight and, now that I'd reached the end of my vanishing time, I felt genuine terror.

Because I didn't know just what was going to happen. Death was one thing, and death was bad enough, but going ghost wasn't death as we know it. It could be anything and it could be a lot worse than the final ending we all have to come to. My imagination played hell with my peace of mind and something of what I feit came through on my expression.

"What's it like, Shellia?" I spoke to the air in a desperate effort to get some sort of comfort. "Does it hurt? Is it the end? Do you know?"

"Stop it!" Carter's hand stung against my cheek. "What the hell's wrong with you? Are you going off the beam?"

"No." I touched my cheek and remembered to act the man.

"Then quit talking to yourself." He frowned. "Shellia? Who's she?"

"A ghost." I wasn't trying to be funny but I'd said the wrong thing and I tasted blood as he struck me in the mouth. He didn't understand. No one could understand who didn't live on vanishing time. If he'd guessed what was to happen he'd have forced me to emerge from hyper-space and head back to Molendis. Or then again he might have used normal drive to try and coast within an inhabited area. I didn't know and I didn't care. All I could do was to wait.

* * * *

While I was waiting I did a lot of thinking. Little things, like the dimming lights, the stuck relay, the indefinable sense of not being alone. It had seemed so easy to talk to Shellia, so natural, and somehow it didn't seem possible that people just winked out of all form of life. An energy shift, the scientists said. A slipping from one end of the matter-spectrum to the other. Perhaps it was the acquiring of a higher entropy, a greater energy potential. If Shellia had dimmed the lights and hindered the power flow through the relay then obviously she could control greater energy than I could. Was she still alive but in a different way? And would I be alive in the same way?

Curtis must have thought so. He had arranged everything and it was safe to assume that both the ship and I would go ghost together. I sat and thought about it, knowing all the time that I was only trying to delude myself and yet, with Carter watching me, it was all I could do.

The ship creaked, the time crawled, my vanishing time disappeared like snow in the summer. Then...

"Nugent!" Carter jerked to his feet, his eyes wild. "Nugent! Where are you?"

I stared at him, then at the outlines of the ship, hazy and somehow unreal. I stood up and stepped forward and found that I was naked. My clothes still lay on the chair behind me. Naturally, they had been new when I left Earth, and, as I stared at them, I knew.

Going ghost was as simple as that. I almost laughed. I almost kissed the man with the gun. Instead I grabbed at it not the least bit surprised to find that I couldn't grasp it. My hand went through it as though it had been mist. Carter stared at the spot where I had been then, even as I watched him, he vanished winked out, disappeared and all around me the ship returned to solid, vibrant life.

Curtis had timed it well. The ship had gone ghost too and, as far as I was concerned, everything was back to normal. Normal that is from my viewpoint. As far as Carter and the others were concerned the ship had simply vanished from around them and left them naked and helpless in hyper-space. I hoped that they hadn't suffered too much.

I turned at the sound of a laugh, remembering my nakedness too late, and then not worrying about it. A girl stood before me, pert, brown-eyed, slim and attractive just as she had appeared in her photograph. And she didn't look sixty years old.

She smiled at me, her eyes warm with understanding and something else. Longing? Loneliness? Love? I didn't know. Explanations could come later.

"Hello, ghost," she said, and stepped forward.

MEMORIES ARE IMPORTANT

Holding it as he did, scant inches from his eyes, the hypodermic held a new and significant importance. Only the instrument was clear, the rest of the room was out of focus, a formless blur against which the machined perfection of glass and chromed steel shone with startling clarity.

Symbolism, thought Carlton absently. The tangible evidence of the advance of science against the unknown, and wondered a little why he, who had long since grown familiar with all the tools of modern medicine, should have entertained such a thought. A little impatient with himself he gently pressed the plunger, watched as a globule of colourless fluid oozed from the slanted tip of the needle, and lowered the instrument. Arden's face replaced the image of the hypodermic.

He was a small man, not young, not old, the only saving feature being his eyes. They glowed in the mediocrity of his face, alive with intelligence, the desperate, unceasing urge to *know*, the eyes of a fanatic. He sat in a chair, loosely dressed in a hospital robe, one sleeve of which was drawn back to reveal his thin, hairless, unmuscular arm.

Carlton stepped forward, pinched up a fold of skin and deftly thrust home the needle. Steadily he pressed the plunger until the barrel was empty, wiping the puncture with alcohol-soaked pad as he withdrew the needle. Arden held the pad in place without being asked, he too was no stranger to the procedure of medicine.

"How long?" The third man in the room leaned forward in his chair. Like the others he was a doctor, like them he was a little more than that. The realm of the mind held, for Hendrickson, a special fascination.

"Several minutes." Carlton gently placed the hypodermic on a surgical table. "We know how the preliminary injection operates, the second stage is the unknown factor."

"Perhaps—" Hendrickson paused. Arden spoke before he could continue.

"Let's not go over all this again," he said. His voice w deep and melodious, the trained tones of a practiced hypnotist. "We have made all the tests we can on animals, now it is time to make the final test. There is only one way."

Hendrickson swallowed, knowing that Arden was right, knowing that what he did had been done before by other men with other drugs but all having a common factor. Caution could only go so far—then had to come the calculated taking of risks. And who better than a skilled observer to take them?

"Odd." Carlton had sat down, his thick, short legs stretched before him, his hands, so big and clumsy looking, and yet so gentle and deft, resting on his thighs. "Have you realised that, if what we hope materialises, all we at present stand for will be obsolete?" He looked from one to the other. "Not surgery, of course, not much of medicine as we know it, but psychiatry will never be the same again."

"So speaks the witch doctor confronted with truth instead of surmise." Arden rubbed his arm, the injection, despite Carlton's care, had bruised the flesh. "Don't overestimate what we are trying to do. We are proving a tool, nothing more. The drug, if it works as we hope, will simply add to the resources of the psychiatrist. It can never replace skill."

Hendrickson nodded, feeling a glow of comfort, recognising why he felt it and then recognised the guilt behind his satisfaction. It isn't easy for anyone to admit that he has served his purpose. For thirty years he had studied to understand some of the workings of the mind, trying to bring help and comfort to the mentally afflicted. The drug, if it worked, would not replace him. His skill would still be necessary and he was glad of it. Then he felt guilty because that meant he, subconsciously, hoped there would still be those needing his assistance. And that, for any psychiatrist, was to suffer guilt. Could he only be happy while others suffered?

* * * *

The room was very quiet. Here, high in one wing of the hospital, away from the wards, the theatre, the now-empty waiting rooms and the out-patients department, the casualty wards and the never-sleeping emergency service, pain and suffering seemed very far away. From the single window the night-scene beneath showed itself as strings of flaring sodium lights, the garish glow of window-signs, the traceries of lighted cars. Even the traffic sounds, muted as they were in the small hours, seemed muffled and distant. Arden's sigh echoed with exaggerated clarity.

At once Carlton was on his feet, his fingers on the other's pulse, his eyes squinting at the dilation of the irises. Arden shook his head.

"Not yet." He restrained his impatience with the older man. "I'll tell you when I'm ready."

"*We'll* tell you when you're ready." Hendrickson made the statement as if it were a joke but he wasn't joking. "You're just a guinea-pig, Arden." He extended the joke.

"What does it feel like to be a laboratory specimen, waiting for the injection that will do—what?"

"We know what it will do!" Arden was sharp. Carlton corrected him.

"We think we know. Later we may be sure, but at the moment all we can do is to hope that we've guessed right."

"Do you guess when you hunt down a trauma and resolve it?" Arden was still sharp. He recognised it and deliberately controlled himself. The drug in his veins made that a simple task—it had been designed to achieve maximum relaxation without any loss of sensual or mental perception. "We know," he continued quietly "that psychosomatic disorders are directly due to mental causes. We know that most mental disorders are due to psychic traumas experienced in childhood. We are certain that, if we can erase these traumas then we can restore mental health and so eliminate psychosomatic disturbances. Agreed?"

There was no disagreement.

"The normal method of psycho-analysis is a long and tedious procedure and, though we may not like to admit it, one with a high percentage of failure. Operative failure, I mean, we know what is wrong but, for one reason or another, be powerless to do anything about it. After all, telling a man that he is ill because of something done to him, before him or with him in his childhood doesn't eliminate it. It doesn't erase it. The memory is still there. Sometimes we can rationalise the memory, give it a new frame of reference, so to speak, but not always. But, if we could remove the memory? Erase it? Then it would, to the individual, never have existed."

It was an old dream. Logically it would provide the cure to the major portion of the world's ills for men un-plagued by disturbing memories would not be driven by the unsuspected devils dictating their actions. Individuals make a state, individuals form a government. Cure the individual and the rest would follow. Eliminate the mischief making memories and happiness would no longer be an unachievable state of existence.

Arden sighed again and now his words came faster as if he were racing time.

"You know what the drug will do. It will cause a complete cessation of memory, temporarily, of course, but effectively. During that period you must confine the activities of the drug to a certain, selected incident..."

His voice droned on but the others were paying more attention to the speaker than to his words. They knew what they had to do. First, when the preliminary injection had taken full effect, to hypnotise Arden so as to bring into the present the selected memory to be erased. Then, with the memory predominant, to administer the drug and so eliminate it. There would be a mental gap which would soon be overlaid with surrounding memories so as to eliminate a vacuum. That wasn't important, it didn't even matter, who can remember, consciously, every incident of an entire lifetime?

They had tried it before, of course, with hypnotism, with electrical shock, with pre-frontal lobotomy, but none had proved satisfactory. Hypnotism blanked out by suggestion but did not erase the memory—it merely raised a barrier artificial and attendant with its own ills. Shock treatment like lobotomy destroyed without selection doing more damage than good. This new drug, if it worked, would replace with a surgeon's scalpel the shotgun effect of present techniques.

"You have my file," said Arden. "A test case but not without personal importance. There was a girl, you know about her. A love affair, over now but not forgotten, how could it ever be forgotten? Years ago and it should be dead but it still lives, still disturbs me, still affects my life." His words came slower, his eyes grew a little vacant, the irises no longer responding quickly to light. He was not asleep, not numbly drugged but he was divorced from immediacy, lost in introspection. "Erase her," he whispered. "Erase her from my mind, from my life. Then, to me, she will never have existed." He sighed, a long deep sigh, and his eyes sharpened a little. "Ready now," he murmured. "Ready…"

Carlton looked at Hendrickson, nodded, rose to his feet and stepped forward towards the surgical table on which lay a second hypodermic and a phial of the new drug. It was transient in effect, there was no need for antidotes, but he wished that he knew more about it. Tests on animals had proved it physically harmless but animals couldn't speak and assessing their intelligence was not an easy task. He remembered several disturbing facts, a guinea-pig who had hunched itself in a corner of its hutch, a rabbit which had consistently beaten its head against a wall, a dog—he preferred not to think about the dog.

But, he reminded himself, Arden was not a dog. He was a reasoning, intelligent man who knew perfectly well what he was doing and who had insisted on doing it. Carlton wondered just how deeply the test-case love affair had affected Arden. Could it, perhaps, have given the impetus to this line of research? Love, even thwarted love, had an unsuspected power.

Carefully he loaded the hypodermic, hardly conscious of Hendrickson's voice as he went through the ritual of expelling all air from the barrel of the instrument. Henrickson's deep, trained, soothing voice loaded with suggestive power, taking Arden back through mental time, winnowing his memories until the desired incident of his first meeting with the girl stood out dominant, skipping forward to find the key note which would ease the hurt most, selecting with the fine Judgment of skill and his thirty years of practice.

Carlton stepped forward, his feet silent on the carpet, the hypodermic ready in his hand, waiting for the moment when Hendrickson, finally satisfied, would give him the signal. It came. Deftly he thrust home the needle, pressed the plunger, withdrew the shining steel.

And, at that moment, a multi-engined jet plane, finding itself in trouble, fought for altitude by a desperate dive towards the sleeping city and a tormented flight upwards away from the serried houses below.

The noise was deafening. The screaming roar of engines and the shattering bang of the sonic wave hit with an almost physical impact. Carlton jumped. Hendrickson obeying instinctive reflex action, turned and sprang to his feet. For a moment neither man was capable of constructive thought.

A moment was enough.

"Arden!"

They thought of him at the same time. They turned from the window which they had instinctively faced and looked towards the chair. Nothing seemed to have altered. Arden still sat as they had last seen him. He hadn't slumped or fallen or died. His eyes were open and he seemed normal.

But he didn't move. He didn't speak. He didn't smile. He hadn't answered to his name. He sat immobile, like an image carved from wax, only the slight lifting of his chest revealing the fact that he was alive, that and the movement of his eyelids as they dropped at regular intervals over his blank, staring empty eyes.

The room hadn't changed. It was still a quiet, warm, somnolent haven in the bustle of the city, a sanctuary which offered privacy and the extended comfort of the womb and that, Hendrickson felt, was all wrong. There should have been damage and disaster, wreckage and shattered glass, ruined plaster and torn brick, devastation to match devastation.

Devastation from which to run, screaming for help, shouting for comfort, the warm understanding of others, the sheer physical need of group effort. He felt panic rise within him and controlled it. He felt sweat beading his face and wiped it with a handkerchief. This devastation, none the less terrible because it was mental, had to be fought alone.

Carlton rose to his feet from where he had squatted before Arden. He looked down at the other man for a moment then sighed. When he spoke it was in almost a whisper, a doctor conferring with a colleague within earshot of his patient.

"No response," he said. "None."

"Catatonia?"

Carlton lifted Ardens arm, placed it above his head, watched as it remained there. Gently he replaced it to its former position.

"Schizophrenia?"

"Obviously. The dissociation must be complete as is the catatonia, you noticed how the voluntary muscular system retained the position in which I placed it." Carlton frowned, deep in thought. "But these are symptoms," he said. "I doubt if Arden is either in true schizophrenia or true catatonia at all. Certainly he hasn't tried to escape from mental stress by reverting back to childhood and there finding more stress and so going back even earlier."

"No foetal position," agreed Hendrickson. "But that isn't conclusive."

"True, but there is another reason. No memories."

And then they had to face it, the thing which, subconsciously, they had both tended to avoid.

* * * *

"The drug erased memory," said Carlton. "I had just injected it when that damn jet made all that noise. You lost contact and Arden must have snapped out of trance. He was fully conscious and aware and then—" He made an expressive gesture. "No memory. None at all."

Hendrickson pursed his lips. "Total amnesia? Surely it must be more than that?"

"A man can lose his memory and still be aware," agreed Carlton. "He may not know who he is or where he comes from or anything but he can still talk and still retain his personality. Arden can't do anything and that is what worries me. The drug must have an unsuspected effect." He remembered the dog, the test animal, and felt himself shudder as he looked at Arden. They had painlessly destroyed the dog—how could they painlessly destroy a man?

"I never did trust that drug," said Hendrickson. "I tried to warn Arden but he was too impatient. Snipping out complete memories sounds good but there has to be a snag." He sounded petulant, a man trying to shift the blame, but Carlton wasn't fooled. Behind those words lay thought processes unconnected with what he was saying. It was a form of verbal doodling; patiently Carlton waited for it to end.

"We've assumed that the drug actually deletes a memory," said Hendrickson. "Something like totally removing a thread from a piece of fabric, but, when you think about it, how can it do that? You just can't remove the cells, and tests show that there is no increase in the electrical emissions of the brain when treated with the drug, no electrical discharge that is. So what happens to the erased memory?"

Carlton shrugged, but made a suggestion.

"Cellular disruption?"

"We found no scar tissue in the test animals even after having been treated with mammoth dosages," reminded Hendrickson. "We know what happens in cases of loss of memory, there is simply a lack of communication, the memories are there but cannot be reached; like books in a library locked away out of sight. But this—" He shook his head as he stared at Arden. "This isn't so simple."

Which, Carlton felt, was an understatement of colossal magnitude. He felt no personal fear because the experiment had slipped control; there have always been men who insist on experimenting on themselves and, aside from some unpleasant publicity, he would not, personally, suffer. Not, that is, if you discount the loss of a friend, the personal conviction of blame and the knowledge that he had helped to destroy a fine mind and brilliant intelligence. He realised that Hendrickson was speaking.

"What did you say?"

"I said, suppose the drug doesn't act exactly as we assumed? Supposing it works in a different way—not by actually destroying the selected memory but by making it impossible to remember?"

"Impossible to remember?" Carlton thought of the dog and, suddenly, it fitted. "That's it! Destroy the ability to remember and the memory is as good as erased." He looked down at Arden, his mind extrapolating the logical results of the concept, and he felt himself grow inwardly cold as he thought about it. "He can't remember a thing," he whispered. "He can't even retain a memory. God! What must it be like?"

* * * *

He opened his eyes and looked at a stranger.

"Arden!" Carlton was desperate with urgency, listen to me…"

The words meant nothing, were just a dull succession of sounds without form or meaning. The stranger vanished, became as if he never was. Before him a wall sprang into being. A window. Darkness beyond the window. His eyes shifted but he knew nothing of the force which had turned his head; the memory of Carlton's hands dissolving as soon as formed. He looked at a corner of a room. A picture. The glowing shade of a lamp. Image following image, each new, each different even though the same, different because seen for the first time.

"Arden!" A man stood before him appearing from nothingness. He moved forward, to Arden it was as if he saw a man, then a man, then a man. He looked at a face which suddenly appeared before him.

"Arden!" Hendrickson was sweating. "Look at me," he ordered. "You know me." His face hung in space. "What's the use," he said hopelessly. "You can't understand."

There was nothing he could understand. There was only a succession of images, a succession of sounds, a total lack of cohesion.

A stranger appearing from nowhere and the word 'you'.

A stranger appearing from nowhere and the word 'can't'.

A stranger appearing from nowhere and the word 'understand'.

Then nothing but blackness, the utter darkness of pre-creation, the deep, engulfing, non-existence of death.

* * * *

Carlton looked at the hypodermic in his hand, then at the slumped figure of Arden.

"I was afraid it wouldn't work," he said. "No reason why it shouldn't, of course, but I'm glad it did."

"Sedation should help," said Hendrickson. He made a sound halfway between a snort and a laugh. "The wonders of modern medicine," he said derisively. "The best panacea is still—simple sleep."

"*Sleep that knits the ravelled sleeve of care,*" quoted Carlton. He put down the hypodermic and then asked defiantly, "What else can we do?"

"Nothing," Hendrickson said. "As I see it we have one hope. The test animals all received overdoses but we insisted on caution with Arden. We know the drug is transient; it has done all the damage it is going to do. Nature has seen to it that we are almost self-repairing. Now we have to wait and give nature a chance."

"In other words we do nothing." Carlton, filled with a sudden restlessness, rose and looked out of the window. Late as it was lights still shone along the streets, glared from the windows in the shopping centre, made brief paths from the lights of the few cars which were always to be found hurrying on their mysterious errands. An ambulance swung into view, slowed as it neared the hospital, vanished as it bore its cargo of suffering into the confines of the building. There would be work and, perhaps, life and death drama in the hospital theatre soon. Strangely it didn't touch him. He felt almost in a world apart.

As Arden, now unconscious, was in a world apart.

Thought of Arden drove him from the window back into his chair. Hendrickson he noticed to his surprise, was asleep in his chair, his head lolling to one side, his mouth open, his breathing stentorian. Carlton toyed with the thought of waking him then, glancing at Arden, dismissed the idea. There was nothing Hendrickson could do. Nothing that either of them could do. Nature had to be given its chance. In the meantime he could only speculate.

Memory, how little they knew about it. Analogies were, at the best, crude and unsatisfactory but it was all they had. Was memory really like a library, the brain a complex filing cabinet, intelligence a means of utilising acquired data? Arden had, temporarily at least, lost the ability to retain a memory. The world, to him was a succession of unrelated images. Carlton tried but found it impossible to imagine what such a world would be like. Sitting, head back against the chair, he did as he had so often done before. He tried to force himself into full empathy with his patient so that, by experiencing what they felt, he could gain understanding of the problems which tormented them.

A world of flashing unrelated images. Things appearing from nowhere, vanishing as if they had never been, new images, always new because unremembered. A being living in an eternal now, no past, no future, only a present.

Chaos. It wouldn't last, it couldn't. The lesions would heal and the mind struggle to repair itself. Inevitably the retention of memory would return—if it did not, then Arden, as a man, would be dead and only a mindless, tormented creature would be in his place. Carlton didn't want to think about it.

Repair then, and a gradual retention of memory. The images would last a little longer, perhaps only as long as Arden concentrated on them. The world would take on a different aspect but, with improvement, would come fresh danger.

Danger. Somehow he knew that he should feel a greater sense of urgency but fatigue claimed him and his thoughts were vague and almost unreal. There would be danger, to Arden, naturally, but how great or how imminent he couldn't, at this time, determine. Later, when he was less tired. Later, when his mind was clear.

He made one last effort to arouse himself and glanced towards Arden. He was still unconscious, safe in his drugged sleep. Carlton sighed and yielded to the force closing his eyes. It was foolish of him to have thought of fear.

Foolish—but his dreams were tormented.

* * * *

"Carlton!"

He stirred, feeling the dryness of his mouth, the ache of his muscles, the grit beneath his eyelids.

"Carlton!" A hand shook him with rough urgency. He opened his eyes, squinting as the harsh light stabbed at them, looked at Hendrickson. Fatigue left him as he saw the other's expression.

"Something wrong?"

"Arden's gone!" Hendrickson stepped back, gestured towards the empty chair. "Vanished! Why the devil didn't you wake me before going to sleep?"

"He was drugged, unconscious…" Carlton broke off his excuse as soon as he recognised it for what it was. "When did you wake?"

"A few moments ago. Something must have woken me, perhaps it was the sound of the door. I saw that Arden had gone and woke you." He paused, frowning. He said; "The door! I thought it was locked?"

It still was.

The door had an old fashioned lock; an inset mortice turned by a key. The key, as Carlton found, was still in his pocket. Blankly he looked at Hendrickson.

"The window!" Together they ran towards it, looked out, knew relief when they saw no huddled body lying in the street five stories below.

"Perhaps he climbed out?"

"In his condition?" Carlton leaned far out of the window, scanning the walls with his eyes. It was getting light, the first pale flush of dawn lightening the sky. In the ghost-grey light the building was clearly visible. Even a trained athlete would have found it impossible to climb from the window—it was an unornamented opening in a smooth expanse of brick.

Carlton's hands were trembling when he closed and locked the window. By all the rules of logic Arden should still be in the room. The door, locked when they had first entered, remained locked, the key in his pocket. The window was impassable. He felt the chill of a mounting panic.

"He could have woken," said Hendrickson. "He could have taken the key from your pocket, opened the door—"

"—locked it and returned the key." Carlton strode impatiently towards the portal, produced the key, unlocked the door. "Remaining in the corridor while he did it."

"All right." Hendrickson had made a mistake and admitted it. "How else?"

"I'm not sure," Carlton hesitated, looking into the corridor outside. "Just before I fell asleep I began to speculate. Something worried me, a sense of danger, a growing fear, I don't know what it was. If I hadn't been so tired I could have worked it out but I was half-asleep and it didn't seem all that important. And I had dreams..." He shook his head "Or were they dreams? But I can make a guess as to how Arden left this room."

"How?"

"He walked through the wall!"

* * * *

The hospital was very quiet. It was still too early for the wards to spring into life, for the patients to be roused, the beds made, temperatures taken, all the smooth, ordered routine of the treatment of the sick. Descending the stairs Carlton had time to explain to Hendrickson what he had meant.

"Memory is more than an accumulation of data; it is, in a sense, a way of life. We all of us have been conditioned to the world in which we live—but not all of us live in the same world. The conditioning, 'memories' of an African primitive, for example, are different to our own. Things we take for granted to him are magic. Magic, to him, can be very real, nonsense to us."

"Social mores," mused Hendrickson. "I'm with you."

"Stay with me." Carlton paused at the foot of a flight of stairs, looked down each arm of a traversing corridor, then continued downward. "Arden cannot retain a memory for more than a short period of time. We must assume that and the evidence proves it. Imagine yourself in such a position. The only reality would be what you could actually see— and that reality would be in a constant state of flux. You would have no sense of permanency, no time-awareness and no orientation. And you would have no taboos."

Words, thought Carlton, were clumsy, things. Even as he ran down the stairs doing his best to explain to Hendrickson, his mind outstripped what he was saying, the mental concepts so beautifully clear. Clear and logical and, as he now knew, inevitable.

Arden had no memories and no ability to retain a memory for more than a short period of time. He saw a wall. A wall with a door. A wall. A door. He didn't know that walls were connected to form a room, that the room had a floor and ceiling, that the door was locked. He didn't know that such a room was an unpassable enclosure. He had no taboos of conditioning, no painful, childhood memories which had 'taught' him that walls were solid, no weight of accepted evidence that a man in such a room could not escape.

And so, because he was free of all tradition and taboos, because he didn't know that he couldn't do it, he had walked from the room.

It was hard to accept. Had Carlton been a mystic it would have been easier, for mystics know nothing is real, all is illusion, all things are, in essence, in the minds of the beholders. And, were they so far wrong?

Close your eyes and, for you, the world ceases to be. Die and, for you, the universe is as if it had never been created. Dismiss a thing from your thoughts and that thing, for you, ceases to exist. Forgetfulness is an erasure, an elimination. Total forgetfulness is a total elimination. Arden had achieved total forgetfulness and now was in the process of creating his own world on the basis of his own experience.

It was the danger which Carlton had sensed and instinctively feared. The thing which now drove him to find Arden before it was too late.

"He's left the hospital." Hendrickson rejoined Carlton, his face shining with perspiration. "The night porter saw him leave. He called to him but Arden didn't answer."

"The idiot!" Carlton was furious. "A man in a hospital gown walks out of the building and the fool didn't think to stop him?"

"He recognised him." It was explanation enough. Inwardly Carlton cursed the student pranks which, to him, were a bane. The porter had thought it odd, naturally but once he had recognised Arden he had made his own assumptions. Various 'rags' had produced odder sights in the past.

But there was no time for recriminations.

Arden had to be found.

* * * *

He was a small, lonely, somehow pathetic figure, the hospital robe loose about his body, stirred slightly by the dawn breeze, his hair ruffled, his slippers incongruous. He stood at the corner of a street not far from the hospital itself and Carlton thanked fate for having allowed them to find him so soon.

"Steady!" He caught hold of Hendrickson's arm. "Have you the hypodermic?"

"Will it be necessary?"

"I think that it will." Carlton halted, staring down the street, thankful that aside from themselves, it seemed deserted. He was not deluded by the apparent helplessness of Arden. The man, though he wasn't aware of it, had greater power than any human. He had to be caught before he could recognise that fact.

"We'll walk softly towards him," ordered Carlton. "As soon as you're within reach use the hypodermic. If anyone bothers us we'll say that he's a patient who is a little mentally confused."

"Why can't we just lead him back?"

Carlton sighed, knowing that, despite his explanations, Hendrickson still hadn't fully grasped what they had to face. Arden had escaped from a locked room simply because he hadn't known that he wasn't supposed to be able to escape from it. It would be as simple for him to escape from human restraint, to move himself at will, to eliminate barriers, to—for want of a better word—perform miracles.

"Now!"

The small figure ahead of them had moved. Arden turned, hesitated, then, suddenly, was on the opposite side of the street and much further down.

"Hurry!" Carlton began to run down the street, his shoes making hard, thudding noises on the pavement. Hendrickson puffed at his side. He had no breath for words but thoughts needed none. He had seen Arden's abrupt move and accepted the need for haste.

"Arden!" Carlton shouted down the street hoping for nothing more than to delay their quarry. "Arden! Wait for us!"

The words, of course, would carry no meaning but their sound, coming as it did from the unknown, might just attract his attention, Might, Carlton hoped, prevent him from moving again in that shockingly abrupt manner. He paused on the verge of shouting again.

Arden had halted close to a lamp standard, his face turned towards the shadowed doorways of the shops lining the street. From one of them a figure emerged. Carlton could guess at the policeman's curiosity.

"Hurry!" he urged Hendrickson. "Hurry!"

Any witness was bad enough but the officer was the last thing he wanted. There would be inquiries, explanations to make with the attendant danger than more would be disclosed than was desirable. But that wasn't the chief cause of Carlton's worry. Arden, with his new attributes, was unpredictable.

Carlton could guess how he made his sudden motions. Arden had no sudden sensation of motion, of walking step by step. It was just that his viewpoint simply altered; the world, literally, changing about him. He had no memory of previous images, no idea of orientation or perspective. He simply went where he wanted to be. Or he fashioned the world as he wished it making distant, small things, large near things. The effect was the same. He had no memory of 'distance' and for him it had no meaning.

And, on the same basis of logic, he could eliminate any scene from his mind simply by wishing it erased.

Carlton didn't want to find out what would actually happen to any object so 'erased.' Nothing, perhaps, there were certain natural forces which might prevent anything drastic happening at all. But Carlton didn't want to find out.

"Get ready," he warned Hendrickson. "No delaying now." And then Arden moved.

And stood just before them.

Hendrickson wasted no time.

* * * *

"We were lucky," Hendrickson said with feeling. "Damn lucky." Carlton, relaxed in his chair, nodded his agreement.

The policeman had been intelligent; too intelligent to believe his eyes. He ignored Arden's abrupt movement, accepted their explanations that he was a mentally deranged patient who had escaped from observation, but had firmly and politely accompanied them back to the hospital. They had been identified, of course, there had been no difficulty about that and, satisfied, the officer had left. There had only remained the task of getting Arden back to his room and the episode was almost over.

Aside from the speculations of the staff, the orderlies, the porters and the wave of rumour which would, even now, be sweeping through the building. But that couldn't be helped and, if Arden recovered, it wouldn't matter.

If he recovered.

Hendrickson voiced Carlton's own, deep-hidden thought.

"You know," he said. "We've hit on something…" he sought for a word "…spectacular."

Carlton remained silent. He was ahead of the other man.

"I've always discounted the extra-sensory perception faculties," continued Hendrickson. "The psi-phenomena, you know what I mean. Well, doesn't this thing prove something."

"It proves quite a lot." Carlton was deliberately non-committal.

"Arden walked out of this locked room. We both saw the way he moved down in the street." He paused, then added casually: "We started an experiment—but it didn't go as expected."

"And you're tempted to let it run its course." Carlton pointed to the figure of Arden, slumped in drugged unconsciousness in his chair. "You're wondering, as I've wondered, just what would happen if we let him alone. I don't know what would happen. I'm only certain of one thing. Arden, as we knew him, would no longer exist."

"I wasn't suggesting—"

"I know." Carlton was tired, he felt the ache of fatigue in his bones. "We have proved, by accident if you like, that memories are more important than we ever guessed. Memory conditions us from the cradle to the grave. We all live in a closed world the boundaries of which are imprinted within us via our memories. We accept those memories and we live by them. We have no choice."

No choice—but now the drug had given them a choice. To erase the entire conditioning of a lifetime so that, for the first time, the mind could be truly free. Free in the one peculiar way Arden had experienced so that no limitations were recognised and, because not recognised, did not exist.

What would be the logical outcome of creating such a freedom?

Carlton didn't know and he didn't want to think about it. He was certain of only one thing. Such a freedom could be achieved only at the cost of the existing personality. The rewards might be high but, for the subject, the price would be too high. The price would be mental death.

He could only hope that Arden had not already paid that price.

Together they set to work. Arden was drugged but they had the entire pharmacopoeia on which to call, drugs for the body and mind, medicines and their years on years of knowledge and, when knowledge failed, the shrewd guesses which all doctors everywhere consider part of their talent.

Carlton, his work done, sat and listened to the soft, soothing, strong and commanding voice of Hendrickson as the expert hypnotist sought to repair the damage of the ravaged mind. He couldn't tell, they had no way of telling how deep were the lesions, how shocking the traumas, how permanent the damage. They could only hope.

Arden had been shocked but his waking periods had been small, most of the time he had been under sedation.

Locked in the blind, dark world of unconsciousness, his mind would have tended to repair itself. Divorced from the new, disturbing stimuli the old channels would have remained open. Now, if their drugs and Hendrickson's suggestions worked, he would wake as if nothing had happened. It took time.

* * * *

The day crawled past, both men eating a hurried meal before returning to their vigil. The window darkened. Fatigue rode them both but they dared not sleep. Lights like stars glowed in the streets below and still Arden did not wake.

"What shall we tell him?" Hendrickson rubbed his eyes, red with his tiredness.

"Nothing. The experiment failed, that's all he needs to know."

"Do you think that he'll be satisfied with that?"

"Perhaps not. If necessary we can explain later." Carlton didn't want to talk about it. Again he considered whether or not to accelerate Arden's waking and for the dozenth time decided against it. They had meddled enough.

In his chair Arden stirred. He sighed, his eyes opening, his face resolving itself into lines and planes as his muscles bunched and his relaxation dissipated. He looked at the two men.

"Carlton." His eyes shifted.

"Hendrickson." He sat, thoughtful, his eyes on the night beyond the window. He sighed again. "So it failed."

"You feel nothing?" Carlton leaned forward.

"Nothing."

Curiosity nagged at Carlton's mind.

"Nothing at all?"

"Nothing to speak of. Just a strange kind of jumbled dream. A peculiar thing…" His voice faded. "But it isn't important."

"No," said Carlton decisively. "It isn't important."

Arden said nothing. His eyes, as they stared at the night, filled with unshed tears. Not because of the failure of the experiment which could have meant so much. But because of the memory of a girl which affected his life. A girl he couldn't forget.

ABOUT THE AUTHOR

English writer E. C. Tubb is internationally known, having been translated into more than a dozen languages. In a sixty-year writing career he published over 120 novels, and more than 200 science fiction short stories in such magazines as *Astounding/Analog*, *Authentic*, *Fantasy Adventures*, *Galaxy*, *Nebula*, *New Worlds*, *Science Fantasy*, and *Vision of Tomorrow*.

Tubb's early science fiction novels were exciting adventure stories, written in the prevailing fashion of the early 1950s. Yet, from his very first novel, his work was characterized at all times by a sense of plausibility, logic, and human insight. These qualities were even more evident in his short stories, which were frequently anthologized.

By 1956 his output included adventure, detective stories, and westerns, but he remained best known for his numerous science fiction novels, of which *Alien Dust* (1955) and *The Space Born* (1956) were acknowledged classics. Tubb became famous for his long-running "Dumarest of Terra" series of novels, the galaxy-spanning saga of Earl Dumarest and his search to find his way back across the stars to the legendary lost planet where he was born—Earth. They eventually spanned thirty-three titles, the final one, *Child of Earth*, appearing in November 2008. Equally well known were his *Space 1999* TV novelizations, and his "Cap Kennedy" novels. Some of his finest SF short stories were collected in *The Best Science Fiction of E. C. Tubb* (Wildside, 2003). Tubb continued to write dynamic science fiction novels right up to his death in October, 2010.

www.ingramcontent.com/pod-product-compliance
Lightning Source LLC
Chambersburg PA
CBHW020146180626
46810CB00004B/1753